THE
CHINESE GOLD MURDERS

ROBERT VAN GULIK

With an Introduction
by
DONALD F. LACH

THE UNIVERSITY OF CHICAGO PRESS
Chicago and London

The University of Chicago Press, Chicago 60637
The University of Chicago Press, Ltd., London

© 1959 by Robert van Gulik
© 1977 by The University of Chicago
All rights reserved. Published 1979
Printed in the United States of America

01 00 99 98 97 96 95 94   6 7 8 9 10

ISBN: 0-226-84864-7
LCN: 79-1536

The Chinese Gold Murders is published by arrangement
with Harper & Row, Publishers, Inc.

CONTENTS

DRAMATIS PERSONAE

It should be noted that in Chinese the surname—here printed in capitals—precedes the personal name.

Main Characters

DEE *Jen-djieh*, newly appointed magistrate of Peng-lai, a town district on the northeast coast of Shan-tung Province. Referred to as "Judge Dee," or "the judge," "the magistrate," etc.

HOONG Liang, Judge Dee's confidential assistant and sergeant of the tribunal. Referred to as "Sergeant Hoong," or "the sergeant."

MA Joong ⎱
CHIAO Tai ⎰ the two trusted assistants of Judge Dee.

TANG, senior scribe of the tribunal of Peng-lai.

Persons connected with "The Case of the Murdered Magistrate"

WANG, Te-hwa, Magistrate of Peng-lai, found poisoned in his library.

YÜ-soo, a Korean prostitute.

YEE Pen, a wealthy shipowner.

Po Kai, his business manager.

Persons connected with "The Case of the Bolting Bride"

KOO Meng-pin, a wealthy shipowner.

MRS. KOO, *née* TSAO, his bride.

TSAO Min, her younger brother.

TSAO Ho-hsien, her father, doctor of philosophy.

KIM Sang, Koo Meng-pin's business manager.

Persons connected with "The Case of the Butchered Bully"

FAN Choong, chief clerk of the tribunal of Peng-lai.

WOO, his manservant.

PEI Chiu, his tenant farmer.

PEI Soo-niang, Pei's daughter.

AH Kwang, a vagabond.

Others

HAI-yüeh, abbot of the White Cloud Temple.

HUI-pen, prior of that temple.

TZU-hai, almoner of that temple.

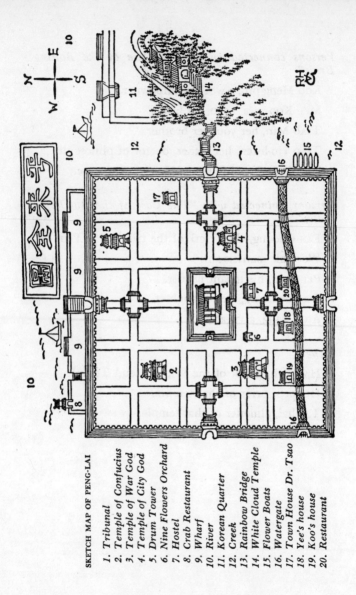

SKETCH MAP OF PENG-LAI

1. Tribunal
2. Temple of Confucius
3. Temple of War God
4. Temple of City God
5. Drum Tower
6. Nine Flowers Orchard
7. Hostel
8. Crab Restaurant
9. Wharf
10. River
11. Korean Quarter
12. Creek
13. Rainbow Bridge
14. White Cloud Temple
15. Flower Boats
16. Watergate
17. Town House Dr. Tsao
18. Yee's house
19. Koo's house
20. Restaurant

PREFACE

The Chinese Gold Murders takes us back to the beginning of Judge Dee's career when, thirty-three years of age, he had been appointed to his first post in the provinces, viz. that of magistrate of Peng-lai, a port city on the northeast coast of Shantung Province.

Then the Tang Emperor Kao-tsung (649–683) had just succeeded in establishing Chinese suzerainty over the greater part of Korea. According to the chronology of *Judge Dee Mysteries,* Judge Dee arrived in Peng-lai in the summer of A.D. 663.* During the successful Chinese Korea campaign in the autumn of the preceding year, when they defeated the combined Korean-Japanese forces, the girl Yü-soo had been carried away as a war slave. Chiao Tai had taken part in the previous campaign of 661 as a captain over hundred.

ROBERT VAN GULIK

---

*In the year 665 Judge Dee was transferred from Peng-lai to Hanyuan, and thence in 668 to Poo-yang in Kiangsu Province. In 670 he was appointed to the magistracy of Lan-fang, on the western frontier, where he stayed five years. In 676 he was transferred to Pei-chow in the far north, where he solved his last three cases as district magistrate. In the same year he was appointed President of the Metropolitan Court of Justice, in the Imperial Capital.

INTRODUCTION

YEARS ago when looking for English materials on life in traditional China, I found the novels, commentaries, and reflections of Lin Yu-tang, Pearl Buck, and Alice Tisdale Hobart very enlightening. Their perceptions, written in charming prose, gently introduced the readers of the 1930s to Chinese society, with its gentry, peasants, and businessmen of the port cities. These writers also translated sensitively certain pieces of popular Chinese literature. Materials of such caliber and character became exceedingly difficult to find in the years following the Second World War, since most Western observers of China, as well as the Chinese themselves, had become obsessed with efforts to explain the decline and fall of the Nationalist government and the rise of the Communists to power. So it was with a sense of relief and satisfaction that readers of the 1950s welcomed the appearance of Robert Hans van Gulik's Judge Dee detective novels, in which imperial China is depicted as a living, identifiable culture rather than as a characterless pawn in the international power game. Because it is no longer possible to recapture the old China by visiting the new, the Dee stories continue to be one of the best available means of recovering a bit of the everyday life of the past.

The career of Van Gulik was a varicolored tapestry woven of threads from the skeins of scholarship, diplomacy, and art. The son of a medical officer of the Netherlands army of Indonesia, he was born in 1910 in Zutphen in Holland's province of Gelderland. Between the ages of three to twelve he lived as a colonial in Indonesia. Upon his family's return to Holland in 1922, young Robert was enrolled in the classical gymnasium (secondary school) at Nijmegen, where his considerable talents for language were quickly recognized. Through C. C. Uhlenbeck, a linguist of Amsterdam University, he was introduced at this early age to the study of Sanskrit and to the language of the Blackfoot Indians of America. In his spare time, he took private lessons in Chinese, his first tutor being a Chinese student of agriculture in Wageningen.

In 1934 Van Gulik attended the University of Leyden, one of Europe's major centers for East Asian studies. Here he worked at Chinese and Japanese systematically but without relinquishing his earlier interest in other Asian languages and literatures. For example, in 1932 he published a Dutch translation of an ancient Indian play written by Kālidasā (ca. A.D. 400). His doctoral dissertation on the horse cult of China, Japan, India, and Tibet, defended at Utrecht in 1934, was published in 1935 by Brill, the publisher of Leyden who specializes in Asian materials. In the meantime Van Gulik also wrote articles for Dutch periodicals on Chinese, Indian, and Indonesian topics; in these articles he first displayed his love for the ancient ways of Asia and his resigned acceptance of the changes taking place.

With his university studies behind him, Van Gulik entered the foreign service of the Netherlands in 1935. His first assignment took him to the legation at Tokyo, where he had an opportunity in off hours to pursue his private scholarly studies. Most of his subjects of inquiry were chosen with reference to the preoccupations of the traditional Chinese literati. His investigations were limited in scope, though rarely in depth, by the time restrictions under which he worked. Like a traditional Chinese gentleman, he himself collected rare books, small objets d'art, scroll paintings, and musical instruments. He also scrutinized his treasures with a scholarship and a connoisseurship that won the respect of leading Oriental collectors. He translated a famous Chinese text by Mi Fu on ink stones, the valued objects on which the calligrapher prepares his ink for writing. He was himself a talented calligrapher, a rare achievement for a Westerner. He played the ancient Chinese lute (*ch'in*) and wrote two monographs about it based on Chinese sources. Most of his publications in these peaceful and seminal years were issued in Peking and Tokyo and won appreciation from both Asian and European scholars.

The holocaust of the Second World War brought an abrupt end to Van Gulik's first Tokyo sojourn. Evacuated in 1942 with other Allied diplomats, he was sent to Chungking as secretary of the Netherlands mission to China. At this remote post he published in 1944 an edition of a rare Chinese work about the Ch'an master Tung-kao, a Buddhist monk who was loyal to the Ming cause in the days of its defeat. He remained in China until the end of the European war in 1945, then returned to The Hague until 1947. The following two years he spent as Councillor of the Dutch embassy in Washington, but in 1949 he finally returned to Japan for a four-year tour of duty.

In 1940 Van Gulik had run across an anonymous eighteenth-century Chinese detective novel that entranced him. Thereafter the vagaries of war and its aftermath cut him off from many of his sources and deprived him of much of his leisure, but he managed to spend odds and ends of free time in studying Chinese popular literature, especially detective and courtroom stories. He prepared an English translation of a traditional detective tale which he published at Tokyo in a limited edition in 1949 under the title *Dee Goong An*. This story in three episodes was the first of the publications through which the Western world learned of the exploits of Judge Dee, one of China's traditional detective heroes.

Van Gulik's fascination with Judge Dee, an exemplar of the imperial magistrate and of the Confucian scholar, led him to further investigations of Chinese jurisprudence and detection. In 1956 he published his English translation of a thirteenth-century case manual called *T'ang-yin pi-shih*.

3

Van Gulik's engrossment with detective literature was soon paralleled by an interest in Chinese erotic literature and art, especially in that of the Ming dynasty (1368–1644). Dalliances with courtesans and concubines were often as much a part of the Chinese gentleman's life as the collecting of ink stones or the playing of the *ch'in*. To demonstrate this point, Van Gulik, always a connoisseur of Chinese pictorial art, published at Tokyo in 1951 a private edition in fifty copies of erotic color prints of the Ming era along with a handwritten essay on the history of Chinese sex life from 206 B.C. to A.D. 1644. While extramarital sex and the popular novel were generally considered off-limits for the Confucian scholar-gentleman, it is clear that many such men relished illicit sex and enjoyed and wrote novels surreptitiously. Through a number of works Van Gulik showed that although the gentlemen of traditional China often gave lip-service to high moral standards, they displayed in their personal lives the moral weakness of people everywhere.

While the erotica published by Van Gulik circulated only to a select audience, his numerous translations and adaptations of Chinese detective stories made Judge Dee famous in the West, especially during the 1950s. Whether posted in New Delhi, The Hague, or Kuala Lumpur, Van Gulik continued to turn out the Judge Dee stories, to a total of at least seventeen. His final diplomatic appointment brought him back to Tokyo in 1965 as the ambassador of the Netherlands to Japan, a post that he had long coveted. Two years later, while on home leave, Van Gulik put down his writing-brush for the last time.

Throughout his relatively short life, Van Gulik found time in the midst of his busy diplomatic career to inquire into an amazing variety of esoteric subjects and to publish his findings. He did not focus upon the great political, social, or economic problems of China, though he was certainly aware of their significance, in touch with the latest scholarly debates, and cognizant of contemporary political events. He did not specialize in a particular period, or even in literature alone, but ranged in his quests from Chinese classical antiquity (ca. 1200 B.C.–A.D. 200) to the end of the Ch'ing dynasty (A.D. 1644–1911). His interest was limited to traditional China rather than to the twentieth-century country with its postimperial and revolutionary struggles. He sought out the "little topics" usually favored by dilettantes and amateurs of arts and letters. To the investigation of these previously unstudied byways he brought his considerable talents as linguist, historian, and connoisseur. While many of his scholarly works appealed to a limited public, his researches into the novel, jurisprudence and crime detection, and erotica were brought to Western popular audiences through his stories about the exploits of Judge Dee, the Sherlock Holmes of China.

Until the present century, the popular Chinese novel was not studied seriously by scholars either in China or in the West. It was in the era between the two world wars that intensive study of Chinese popular literature began. In the aftermath of the Chinese revolution of 1911–12 and of the disruptions brought on by the First World War, the new literati of Republican China sought to establish the spoken language (*pai-hua*) as the general language in order to help modernize the country. The leaders of this radical literary renaissance—Hu Shih, Lu Hsün, and Ts'ai Yüan-p'ei—began to revive the popular literature of the past in the hope of showing that the spoken language had been, and so might be to a greater extent in the future, a sturdy vehicle of literary expression. Because they were also eager to provide new reading matter for the masses, they looked to the past for appealing tales, intricate plots, and moral examples which could be reissued or refurbished for the public. As recently as 1975, Chinese archeologists uncovered in Hupeh Province a cache of bamboo books from the Ch'in dynasty (221–207 B.C.) which reportedly include materials on crime and detection as well as popular accounts of the magistrate as detective. Thus the search for the origins of the crime novel is being continued.

The Japanese literati, who were not as prejudiced against popular literature as their Chinese contemporaries, had long collected Chinese popular dramas and stories and had sometimes adapted them to Japanese tastes before publishing new editions. Western scholars, especially the French school of sinologues exemplified in our century by Paul Pelliot, had studied Chinese legend and story before the reforming scholars of the Chinese Republic became alert to their importance as mediums of political instruction and propaganda. In the 1930's the Chinese Communists likewise became aware of the significance of popular drama for propaganda; nor have they lost that awareness since taking over the government in 1949.

Van Gulik, a product of the European sinological school dominated by Pelliot, shared that school's enthusiasm for comparative studies and exotic subjects. For this breed of scholars, the smallest and most esoteric topics became broadly meaningful through the extraordinary linguistic, literary, and artistic analyses and perceptions of the investigator. In short, the subject was given importance, substance, and relevance by the imaginative powers and talents of the researcher. When Van Gulik first arrived in Japan in 1935, he was quick to see that its artistic collections and libraries were rich in the materials of Chinese popular culture. As an imaginative scholar with limited time at his disposal, Van Gulik immediately realized that he could produce fascinating studies of the culture of the Chinese gentry through intensive study of the objects which those privileged people collected and the customs they observed.

The Chinese crime or courtroom novel was a later form of one of the main genres of the colloquial narrative tradition—the detective story. From the time of the Sung dynasty (A.D. 960-1279), and probably much earlier, the common people delighted in listening to the tales of the storytellers who per-

formed in the bazaars or on the streets of cities and towns. One of the popular detective heroes of the storytellers was Judge Dee (Ti Jen-chieh), a historical personage and statesman of the T'ang court who lived from A.D. 630 to 700. He and other magistrates, especially Pao Cheng (A.D. 999–1062), were celebrated by storytellers, dramatists, and novelists. In the process the historical deeds of the judge became the basis for legendary accomplishments in detection, unswervingly right conduct, and superhuman insight. The judge-detective became the central figure of a stereotype that permeated all forms of popular literature.

The hero of the traditional Chinese detective novel is normally a local magistrate. The story is usually told in colloquial language from the point of view of the working magistrate, who acts as detective, inquisitor, judge, and public avenger. It ordinarily involves a number of crimes, for the magistrate rarely had the leisure or opportunity to deal with one crime at a time. The crimes normally occur early in the story and are often interrelated. Usually the plays or stories are not didactic, and involve crimes against the person rather than misdeeds against society. The crime is always a specific infraction of statute law, ordinarily murder or rape or both. The judge acts as the instrument of the state or the emperor in establishing the facts of the case, capturing the criminal, and meting out the punishments prescribed by law. There is almost no place in the traditional stories for the judge personally to exercise discretion, extend mercy, or play favorites. The judge exemplifies courage, sagacity, honesty, impartiality, and severity; he possesses a flair for detection which is sometimes aided by superhuman insights or by knowledge conveyed to him by ghosts directly from the netherworld. Humor and lightness are rarely associated with the judge, though his subordinates sometimes become involved in clownish escapades.

The judge, always a middle-aged male of the literary class, is disdainful of luxury, protective of the weak or wronged, and

above corruption and flattery. The criminal, especially the murderer, is usually cold-blooded and irredeemably evil, requires several beatings to confess, and deserves the awful punishments prescribed by law. The criminal may be of any age or class and of either sex. Tartars, Mongols, Taoists, and Buddhists are almost always cast as miscreants. The victim ordinarily belongs to the artisan class, as did most of the audience.

A rudimentary theme of social justice runs through the stories. In imperial China the administration of justice aimed at retribution and the redress of wrongs; a magistrate dutifully and correctly performs these functions as he keeps the affairs of this earth in harmony with the will of Heaven. All trials were held in the courtroom and could be viewed by the public. The prosecuting judge had to question the accused in open court and never in private. While the judge himself was thought to recognize guilt or innocence intuitively and immediately, he was required to prove his case in public and had to force a confession from the accused. All the proceedings were carefully written down for the record, and the accused had to verify the accuracy of the transcript by signing it. Because criminals were often sly, the judge was sometimes confused, though never more than momentarily. Although most of the investigation was conducted by bailiffs, the judge, in the interests of efficiency or justice would sometimes make a personal investigation. The public, both in the street and in the courtroom, criticized or praised the activities and decisions of the judge. If the people suspected the judge of corruption, favoritism, or wrong-headedness, public protests and disorders were expected to follow. If a magistrate's superiors became convinced of his wrongdoing, he was dismissed and punished; if a public protest was adjudged wrong and seditious, an entire district would be punished.

When Van Gulik published his first translation of a Judge Dee story in 1949, he suggested that a modern writer of detective stories might try his hand at a novel in the Chinese mode for

the day's readers. Because nobody accepted this challenge, Van Gulik decided to undertake the task himself, even though he had no previous experience in writing fiction. Originally he intended to show the reading public of Japan and China how much better the traditional stories were than those translated from Western originals then being sold in the stalls of Tokyo and Shanghai. He wrote his first two novels in English as working drafts for versions that he intended ultimately to publish in Japanese and Chinese. When his Western friends exhibited enthusiasm for this new type of detective story, he decided to continue writing in English, another foreign language in which he had become highly proficient.

The giant step from scholarly research and translation to imaginative writing was one that Van Gulik made decisively and successfully. His former involvement with unfrequented paths of scholarly research proved to be splendid preparation for his leap into the writing of atmospheric Chinese detective stories. Now it was no longer necessary to stick to precise historical facts and texts; accuracy of background and realistic portrayal of life in traditional China had become paramount. While using Judge Dee as a stock character, Van Gulik could draw freely upon the plots, stories, and data offered by the whole body of Chinese literature. And to these he could easily add fascinating and titillating embellishments from his own scholarly researches and reading. He also enlivened the novels with his own imaginary maps and with his drawings of Chinese scenes based on sixteenth-century pictorial block prints.

Van Gulik's earlier Judge Dee stories, prepared between 1950 and 1958, are closer to Chinese originals than are those he wrote subsequently. Five in number, these early novels include *The Chinese Bell Murders* and *The Chinese Nail Murders* now reproduced in new editions. Van Gulik wrote the *Bell Murders* in Tokyo during 1950 as the first of his efforts; the *Nail Murders* he wrote in Beirut in 1956. He ordinarily chose his plots and characters while relaxing from official duties, and laid out the preliminary topography as he prepared a map of an imaginary city. In the *Bell Murders* all three plots were taken directly from Chinese stories; in the other Judge Dee books Van Gulik himself supplied most of the themes and plots. Once the actual writing began, it normally took him about six weeks to complete a novel.

From the beginning Van Gulik was aware of the limitations of traditional Chinese prose fiction. Stories of murder, adultery, mystery, and violence were sure to appeal to a Western audience which never seemed to be sated by such offerings. But other features of Chinese colloquial fiction were not likely to be so well received. The criminal's identity was ordinarily revealed at the beginning of Chinese stories; out of deference to Western custom Van Gulik puts the solution near the end. Chinese materials were too often drawn from unfamiliar customs and beliefs, and Chinese authors too often content to solve a puzzling mystery by calling for supernatural knowledge or intervention. Where Westerners would expect morals to be drawn or motivations clarified, the Chinese authors rarely made these matters explicit. Character portrayal in Chinese novels was often limited to depiction of social types. Practically no effort was made to analyze or develop individual character and to evaluate the influence of environment or background upon it.

Judge Dee himself, as depicted in the Chinese stories, was a character utterly foreign to Westerners. To make him more credible Van Gulik sought to make him more human. Occasionally he smiles, becomes excited in the presence of an attractive woman, or feels unsure of himself and his decisions. Van Gulik also plays down Dee's strict Confucian view of the world, which included an unshakable faith in the superiority of everything Chinese and a disdain for all foreigners, a steadfast belief in all aspects of filial piety, a matter-of-fact attitude toward torture, and an unrelenting hostility to Buddhism and Taoism.

While he could not completely ignore these traditional attributes, Van Gulik preferred to soften his Judge's attitudes and to add to his human dimension by making him a devoted family man, a connoisseur of arts and letters, and a deeply religious person. Normally the Judge also tries to solve crimes rationally and without intervention at critical moments from the netherworld.

While consciously adapting his stories to the Western audience, Van Gulik preserved extraordinarily well the way of life of imperial China. The reader will appreciate the part played in that society by family when Dee chastizes the father for not watching more closely over the virtue of his daughter. He will come to understand the role of the student, his privileges and responsibilities to society, and the relation of education to morality. He will also learn from Dee that Buddhist monks typically lust for women and are crafty in politics, that Tartars are untrustworthy and, like Taoists, given to black magic, and that southerners differ greatly from northerners in spoken language and customs. The smallest items—ink stones, nails in a Tartar shoe, the gongs of Taoist monks, door knobs—are brought into the stories at strategic points in the plot to give Van Gulik the opportunity to enlighten the Western reader about these strange objects and their functions. No foreign reader can escape a feeling for the importance in China of the written language and of written records and documents; for the prevalence of social corporations unfamiliar to Westerners, such as the Beggar's Guild; or for the exaggerated concern with proper ceremony and polite forms of address. The seamy side of life is also exposed by reference to the sale of female children into slavery and by the prevalence of prostitution. Asides on foreign trade, on the imperial salt monopoly, on "squeeze" or petty bribery, and on cooking add to the realism of the stories. The role of women is depicted as limited to homemaking, sex, handicrafts, and childrearing.

The Judge Dee stories should not be taken as completely accurate depictions of life in imperial China. For one thing, they are anachronistic. The historical Judge Dee lived in the seventh century, but most of the Chinese stories about him were written down in the sixteenth to nineteenth centuries and reflect the standards and practices current then. Van Gulik based his adaptations on these later collections. Although he was a close student of the Ming and Ch'ing dynasties, the Dutch scholar's experiences with life in China were limited to a few brief visits and to several years' stay during the Second World War. He idealizes the China which existed before the empire had been shaken by the disruptive influences of the West and Japan. He sees imperial China most often from the viewpoint of the Confucian gentry for whose way of life he had respect and affection.

Still, these stories, for all their limitations and biases, provide relatively accurate portrayals of certain aspects of everyday life in imperial China. Van Gulik's personal observations were made in a pre-Communist era when the old ways were still followed in the villages and towns and when the magistrate was still dominant in local affairs. Highly sensitive to the stuff of everyday life, Van Gulik was not an ordinary observer of the Chinese scene. From his studies and his experience with the highest echelons of government he acquired qualifications for understanding traditional China that are no longer part of the equipment of specialists. No amount of reading in classical texts, gazeteers, dynastic histories, or diplomatic documents will by itself provide depth of understanding about the basic workings of life in traditional China. For the Westerner, direct translations of Chinese popular tales are often too foreign in nature and leave references to common matters too frequently unexplained for full comprehension. The insights and elucidations offered by Van Gulik provide the Westerner with a painless and pleasant introduction to premodern China and with an understanding of how different, yet sometimes how similar, are the peoples and societies of China and the West. And, besides, these are entertaining stories and should be appreciated simply for their own sake.

Donald F. Lach

FOR FURTHER READING

"Necrology of R. H. van Gulik (1910–1967)." *T'oung pao* 54 (1968): 116–24. Unsigned but probably by A. F. P. Hulsewe. At the end of the article appears a comprehensive but incomplete bibliography of Van Gulik's works, including the Judge Dee books.

Bishop, John L. "Some Limitations of Chinese Fiction." *Studies in Chinese Literature*, Harvard-Yenching Institute Studies, no. 21, pp. 237–45. Cambridge, Mass., 1966.

Hayden, George A. "The Judge Pao Plays of the Yüan Dynasty." Ph.D. dissertation, Stanford University, 1972.

Lin Yu-tang. *Lady Wu: A True Story*. London, 1937. A historical biography in which Judge Dee (here written "Di") figures.

Prousek, J. "Researches into the Beginnings of the Chinese Popular Novel." *Archiv Orientální* (Prague) 11 (1939): 91–132.

Shih Chung-wen. *The Golden Age of Chinese Drama: Yüan Tsachü*. Princeton 1976. Note especially pp. 100–112, on social justice in the courtroom stories.

Starrett, Vincent. "Some Chinese Detective Stories." In *Bookman's Holiday*, pp. 3–26. New York, 1942.

Van Gulik, Robert H. "Bibliography of Dr. R. H. van Gulik." Reproduced typescript. Boston [ca. 1970]. Compiled for the benefit of the Boston University Libraries—Mugar Memorial Library "Robert van Gulik Collection."

See also the postscripts to the various Judge Dee books, in which Van Gulik discusses the traditional Chinese system of justice, his sources for the Dee stories, and his working methods.

ONE.

THREE OLD FRIENDS PART IN A COUN-TRY PAVILION; A MAGISTRATE MEETS TWO HIGHWAYMEN ON THE ROAD

Meeting and parting are constant in this incon-
stant world,
Where joy and sadness alternate like night and
day;
Officials come and go, but justice and righteous-
ness remain,
And unchangeable remains forever the imperial
way.

Three men were silently sipping their wine on the top floor of the Pavilion of Joy and Sadness, overlooking the highway crossing outside the north gate of the imperial capital. Ever since people could remember, this old, three-storied restaurant, built on a pine-clad hillock, had been the traditional place where metropolitan officials were wont to see off their friends leaving for posts in the interior, and where they came again to bid them welcome when, their term of office completed, they returned to the capital. As indicated in the above-quoted poem engraved on its main gate, the pavilion derived its name from this double function.

The sky was overcast, the spring rain was coming down in a dreary drizzle that looked as if it would never cease. Two workmen in the cemetery down at the back of the hillock had sought shelter under an old pine tree, huddling close together.

The three friends had partaken of a simple noon meal; now the time of parting was drawing near. The difficult last moments had come, when one gropes in vain for the right words. All three were about thirty years old. Two wore the brocade caps of junior secretaries; the third, whom they were seeing off, the black cap of a district magistrate.

Secretary Liang put down his wine cup with a determined gesture. He said testily to the young magistrate, "It's the fact that it's so completely unnecessary that irks me most! You had the post of junior secretary in the Metropolitan Court of Justice for the asking! Then you would have become a colleague of our friend Hou here, we could have continued our pleasant life together here in the capital, and you—"

Magistrate Dee had been tugging impatiently at his long, coal-black beard. Now he interrupted sharply.

"We have been over this many times already, and I—" He quickly caught himself up and went on with an apologetic smile, "I told you that I am sick and tired of studying criminal cases—on paper!"

"There is no need to leave the capital for that," Secretary Liang remarked. "Aren't there enough interesting cases here? What about that secretary of the Board of Finance, Wang Yuan-te his name is, I think, the fellow who murdered his clerk and absconded with thirty gold bars from the Treasury? Our friend's uncle Hou Kwang, secretary-general of the Board, asks the Court every day for news, isn't it, Hou?"

The third man, who wore the insignia of a secretary of the Metropolitan Court, looked worried. He hesitated somewhat, then replied, "We haven't got a single clue yet to that scoundrel's whereabouts. It's an interesting case, Dee!"

"As you know," Magistrate Dee said indifferently,

"that case has the personal attention of the president of the Court himself. All you and I have seen of it to date is a few routine documents, copies! Paper, and more paper!"

He reached for the pewter wine jug and refilled his cup. All were silent. After a pause Secretary Liang spoke.

"You could at least have chosen a better district than Peng-lai, that dismal place of mist and rain, far away on the seacoast! Don't you know the weird stories they tell about that region since olden times? They say that on stormy nights the dead rise there from their graves, and strange shapes flit about in the mist that blows in from the ocean. They even say that weretigers are still slinking about in the woods there. And to step in the shoes of a murdered man! Everyone in his senses would have refused that post, if it were offered to him, but you even asked for it!"

The young magistrate had hardly listened to him. Now he said eagerly, "Think of it, a mysterious murder to solve, right after one has arrived at one's post! To have an opportunity right away for getting rid of dry-as-dust theorizing and paper work! At last I'll be dealing with men, my friends, real, living men!"

"Don't forget the dead man you'll have to deal with," Secretary Hou remarked dryly. "The investigator sent to Peng-lai reported that there was no clue to the murderer of the magistrate, nor to the criminal's motive. And I told you already that part of the file on that murder unaccountably disappeared from our Court's archives, didn't I?"

"The implications of that fact," Secretary Liang added quickly, "you know as well as we! It means that the magistrate's murder has ramifications here in the capital. Heaven knows what hornets' nest you are going to stir up, and what intrigues of high officials you'll get involved in! You have passed all the literary examinations with honors; here in the capital you have a great future before you. And you prefer to bury yourself in that lonely place, Peng-lai!"

"I advise you, Dee," the third young official said earnestly, "to reconsider your decision. There is still time; you could easily plead a sudden indisposition and ask for ten days' sick leave. In the meantime they'll assign another man to that post. Do listen to me, Dee. I am speaking to you as your friend!"

Magistrate Dee noticed the look of entreaty in his friend's eyes. He felt deeply touched. He had known Hou only for a year, but had formed a high opinion of his brilliant mind and his exceptional capacities. He emptied his wine cup and rose.

"I appreciate your solicitude as a further mark of your staunch friendship!" he said with a warm smile. "Both of you are perfectly right, it would be better for my career if I stayed on in the capital. But I owe it to myself to go on with this undertaking. The literary examinations Liang referred to just now I consider as routine; I feel that they don't count for me. And neither do I count the years of paper work I have had in the Metropolitan Archives here. I have yet to prove to myself that I am really capable of serving our illustrious emperor and our great people. The magistracy of Peng-lai is the real beginning of my career!"

"Or the end," Hou muttered under his breath. He rose also and walked to the window. The gravediggers had left their shelter and were starting their work. He grew pale and quickly glanced away. Turning round he said hoarsely, "The rain has stopped."

"Then I'd better go!" Magistrate Dee exclaimed.

Together the three friends descended the narrow, winding staircase.

In the courtyard below an elderly man stood waiting with two horses. The waiter filled the stirrup cup. The three friends emptied it in one draught, then there

18

were the confused last messages and wishes. The magistrate swung himself into the saddle; the graybeard ascended the other horse. Magistrate Dee waved his whip in farewell, then the pair rode down the path that led to the highway.

As Secretary Liang and his friend Hou stood looking after them, the latter said with a worried look, "I didn't like to tell Dee, but this morning a man from Peng-lai told me about queer rumors there. They are saying that the ghost of the murdered magistrate has been seen walking in the tribunal."

Two days later, toward noon, Magistrate Dee and his assistant reached the border of Shantung Province. They had their noon meal in the military post, changed their horses, then went on eastward along the highway to Peng-lai. The road led through a thickly wooded, hilly country.

The magistrate wore a simple brown traveling dress. His official costume and a few personal belongings he carried in two capacious saddlebags. Since he had decided that his two wives and his children should follow him later, after he had settled down in Peng-lai, he could afford to travel light. Later his family would bring along his other possessions and his servants in tilt carts. His assistant, Hoong Liang, carried the magistrate's two most prized possessions, the famous sword Rain Dragon, an heirloom of the Dee family, and the old standard work on jurisprudence and detection, in the margins of which Dee's late father, the imperial councilor, had added copious notes in his precise handwriting.

Hoong Liang was an old retainer of the Dee family in Tai-yuan; he had looked after the magistrate when he was still a child. Later, when the magistrate had moved to the capital and set up his own household there, the loyal old servant had accompanied him. He

19

had made himself very useful helping in supervising the household, at the same time acting as Dee's confidential secretary. And now he had insisted on following his master to Peng-lai, his first post in the provinces.

Letting his horse step in an easy gait, the magistrate turned round in his saddle and said, "If we keep this dry weather, Hoong, we should arrive tonight at the garrison city of Yen-chow. We can start from there early tomorrow morning, so that we reach Peng-lai in the afternoon."

Hoong nodded.

"We shall ask the commander at Yen-chow," he said, "to send an express messenger ahead, to apprise the tribunal of Peng-lai of our impending arrival, and—"

"We'll do nothing of the sort, Hoong!" the other interrupted quickly. "The senior scribe, who, after the murder of the magistrate there, was temporarily charged with the administration, knows that I have been appointed, and that's enough! I prefer to arrive unexpectedly. That's also why I refused the military escort the commander of the boundary post offered me."

As Hoong remained silent, his master continued.

"I carefully studied the file of the magistrate's murder, but as you know the most important part is missing, namely the private papers found in the dead man's library. The investigator brought them back with him to the capital, but they were stolen."

"Why," Hoong asked worriedly, "did the investigator stay only three days in Peng-lai? After all, the murder of an imperial magistrate is no small matter; he should have devoted more time to the case, and not have left there without at least having formulated a theory about how and why the crime was committed."

Magistrate Dee nodded eagerly.

"And that," he remarked, "is only one of the many curious aspects of the case! The investigator reported only that Magistrate Wang had been found poisoned in his library, that the poison had been identified as the powdered root of the snake tree, that it was not known how that poison had been administered, and that there were no clues to the criminal, nor to his motive. That was all!"

After a while he continued. "As soon as the papers of my appointment had been signed, I went to the Court to call on the investigator. But I found he had left already on a new assignment far down in the south. His secretary gave me the incomplete dossier. He said that the investigator had not discussed the case with him, that he had left no notes on it, and no oral instructions as to how he thought the case should be handled. So you see, Hoong, we'll have to start from scratch!"

The graybeard did not answer; he did not share his master's enthusiasm. They rode on in silence. Since some time now they had met no other travelers. They were traversing a wild stretch of country; high trees and thick undergrowth lined the road on both sides.

After they had turned a bend, suddenly two men on horseback emerged from a narrow side path. They wore patched riding jackets, and their hair was bound up with dirty blue rags. While one aimed the arrow on his crossbow at the travelers, the other rode up to them, a drawn sword in his hand.

"Get down from your horse, official!" he shouted. "We'll accept yours and that of the old man as a courtesy of the road!"

TWO.

A STRENUOUS SWORD DUEL IS BROKEN
OFF UNDECIDED; FOUR MEN DRINK
WINE IN THE HOSTEL OF YEN-CHOW

Hoong quickly turned around in his saddle to hand his master his sword. But an arrow swished past his head.

"Leave the toothpick alone, old man!" the archer shouted. "The next arrow goes right into your throat!"

Magistrate Dee quickly surveyed the situation. Angrily biting his lip, he saw there was little he could do; they had been taken completely by surprise. He cursed himself for not having accepted the military escort.

"Hurry up," the first ruffian growled. "Be grateful that we are honest highwaymen, who let you off with your life."

"Honest highwaymen!" the magistrate said with a sneer as he climbed down from his horse. "Attacking an unarmed man, and that with an archer to cover you! You two are just a couple of common horse thieves!"

The man jumped from his horse with amazing quickness and stood himself in front of the magistrate, his sword ready. He topped him by an inch; his broad shoulders and thick neck showed him to be a man of extraordinary strength. Pushing his heavy-jowled face forward he hissed, "You can't insult me, dog-official!"

Magistrate Dee's face went scarlet. "Give me my sword!" he ordered Hoong.

The archer drove his horse immediately in front of the graybeard.

"Keep your mouth shut and do as you are told!" he said threateningly to the magistrate.

"Prove that you aren't just a couple of thieves!" the magistrate snapped. "Hand me my sword. I'll first finish off this rascal and then settle with you!"

The big man with the sword suddenly guffawed. Putting his sword down, he called out to the archer, "Let's have a little joke with the beard, brother! Let him take his sword, I'll cut him up a bit to teach that brush-wielder a lesson!"

The other gave the magistrate a thoughtful look.

"There's no time for jokes!" he said sharply to his companion. "Let's take the horses and be gone."

"Just as I thought," Magistrate Dee said contemptuously. "Big words but small hearts!"

The large man cursed violently. He stepped up to Hoong's horse, grabbed the sword the graybeard was carrying and threw it to the magistrate, who caught it and quickly took off his traveling robe. He parted his long beard and knotted the two strands together behind his neck. Drawing his sword, he said to the ruffian, "Whatever happens you'll let the old man go free!"

The other nodded, then at once attacked with a quick thrust at the magistrate's breast. He easily parried it, then followed up with a few swift feints that made the ruffian fall back with a gasp. The man now attacked with greater caution, and the sword duel began in earnest, Hoong and the archer looking on. As they exchanged blow for blow the magistrate noticed that his opponent had apparently learned the art by actual practice; his fencing lacked the finer points of the schooled swordsman. But he was a man of formidable strength, and showed himself a clever tactician by enticing Dee repeatedly to the rough ground by the roadside, where the magistrate had to pay much atten-

23

tion to his footwork. This was the magistrate's first real fight outside the training hall, and he thoroughly enjoyed it. He thought that before long he would get a chance to disable his opponent. But the other's common sword could not stand up so long against the tempered blade of Rain Dragon. When the ruffian parried a sharp blow, his sword suddenly snapped in two.

As the man stood there looking dumbfounded at the stump in his hand, Magistrate Dee turned to the other.

"Your turn!" he barked.

The archer jumped from his horse. He took off his riding jacket and tucked the slips of his robe under his belt. He had seen that the magistrate was a first-class fencer. But after a swift exchange of thrusts and counterthrusts the magistrate also knew that this was a dangerous opponent, a schooled sword fighter, with whom one could take no chances. The magistrate felt thrilled. The first fight had loosened his limbs; now he felt in perfect condition. The sword Rain Dragon felt like a part of his own body. He went for his opponent with a complicated combination of feints and hits. The other sidestepped—he was surprisingly light on his feet for a man of his bulk—and counterattacked with a succession of quick cuts. But the sword Rain Dragon swished through the air; it parried each of the thrusts, then shot out in a long stab that missed the other's throat by the fraction of an inch. The man didn't flinch; he quickly made a few feints preparatory to a new attack.

Suddenly there was a loud clang of arms. A group of twenty horsemen came round the bend and quickly surrounded the four men. They were heavily armed with crossbows, swords and pikes.

"What is going on here?" their leader shouted. The short mail jacket and the spiked helmet proclaimed him a captain of the mounted military police.

Annoyed at this interruption of his first real sword duel, the magistrate replied curtly, "I am Dee Jen-djieh, newly appointed magistrate of Peng-lai. These three men are my assistants. We had a long ride, and are engaging in a friendly bout of fencing to stretch our stiff legs."

The captain gave them a dubious look.

"I'll trouble you for your papers, magistrate," he said in a clipped voice.

Magistrate Dee pulled an envelope from his boot and gave it to the captain. He quickly glanced through the documents inside, then gave them back and saluted.

"I regret to have bothered you, sir," he said politely. "We got a report that there are highwaymen about here, so I have to be careful. Good luck!"

He barked a command at his men, and they galloped away.

When they had disappeared from sight, the magistrate raised his sword.

"We go on!" he said, and aimed a long thrust at his opponent's breast. The other parried the blow, then held up his sword, and put it back in its scabbard.

"Ride on to your destination, magistrate," he said gruffly. "I am glad there are still officials like you in our empire."

He gave a sign to the other. They jumped on their horses. Magistrate Dee gave his sword to Hoong, and started to put on his robe again.

"I take my words back," he said curtly. "You are indeed highwaymen. But if you go on like this, you'll end up on the scaffold like common thieves. Whatever your grudge is, forget it. There's news about heavy fighting with the barbarians up north. Our army needs men like you."

The archer shot him a quick look.

"And my advice to you, magistrate," he said calmly, "is that you carry your sword yourself, else you'll be caught unawares again."

He turned his horse round, and the two disappeared among the trees.

As Magistrate Dee took his sword from Hoong and hung it over his own back, the old man said contentedly, "You gave them a good lesson, sir. What kind of people would those two have been?"

"Usually," the magistrate replied, "it is men with some real or imagined grudge who choose to become outlaws. But their code is to rob only officials and wealthy people; they often help people in distress, and they have a reputation for courage and chivalry. They call themselves 'brothers of the green woods.' Well, Hoong, it was a good fight, but we have lost time. Let's hurry on."

They entered Yen-chow at dusk, and were directed by the guards at the gate to the large hostel for traveling officials in the center of the town. Magistrate Dee took a room on the second floor, and ordered the waiter to bring them a good meal, for he felt hungry after the long journey.

When they had finished their meal, Hoong poured out a cup of hot tea for his master. Dee sat down near the window and looked out on the place below, in front of the hostel, where there was a busy coming and going of lance-knights and footmen. The light of torches shone on their iron helmets and breastplates.

Suddenly there came a knock on the door. Turning round, the magistrate saw two tall men enter the room.

"August heaven!" he exclaimed, astonished. "Here we have our two brothers of the green woods!"

The two bowed awkwardly. They still wore their patched riding jackets, but now they had hunting caps on their heads. The burly fellow who had attacked them first spoke. "Sir, this afternoon on the road you told that captain that we were your assistants. I talked this over with my friend, sir, and we agreed that we wouldn't like to make you a liar, you being a magistrate. If you'll take us on, we'll serve you loyally."

The magistrate raised his eyebrows. The other man said hurriedly, "We know nothing of the work in a tribunal, sir, but we know how to obey orders, and we thought we could perhaps make ourselves useful by doing the rough work for you."

"Take a seat," Magistrate Dee said curtly. "I'll hear your stories."

The two sat down on footstools. The first laid his big fists on his knees, cleared his throat and began.

"My name is Ma Joong, I am a native of Kiangsu Province. My father owned a cargo junk, and I helped him as mate. But since I was a strong boy who liked fighting, my father sent me to a well-known boxing master, and had him teach me also some reading and writing, so as to qualify for becoming an officer in the army. Then my father died unexpectedly. Since there were many debts, I had to sell our boat, and entered the service of the local magistrate, as his bodyguard. I soon found out that he was a cruel and corrupt scoundrel. Once he cheated a widow out of her property by extracting a false confession from her by torture. I quarreled with him and he made to strike me. Then I knocked him down. I had to flee for my life and took to the woods. But I swear by the memory of my dead father that I never wantonly killed a man, and robbed only those who could afford the loss. You can take my word for it that the same goes for my blood brother here. That's all!"

Magistrate Dee nodded, then looked questioningly at the other man. He had a finely chiseled face, a straight nose and thin lips. Fingering his small mustache, he said, "I call myself Chiao Tai, because my real family name is well and honorably known in a certain part of the empire. A high official once willfully sent a number of my comrades for whom I was respon-

sible to their death. The scoundrel disappeared, and
the authorities to whom I reported his crime refused
to take action. Then I became a highwayman, and
roamed all over our empire, hoping one day to trace
the criminal and kill him. I never robbed the poor, and
my sword is unsullied by unjust blood. I'll serve you on
one condition, namely that you'll allow me to resign
as soon as I have found my man. For I have sworn by
the souls of my dead comrades that I would cut off his
head and throw it to the dogs."

The magistrate looked intently at the two men in
front of him, slowly caressing his side whiskers. After
a while he said, "I'll accept your offer, including Chiao
Tai's condition—on the understanding that, should he
find his man, he'll first give me an opportunity for trying to redress his wrong by legal means. You can go
with me to Peng-lai, and I'll see whether I can use you.
If not, I'll tell you so, and you'll promise then to have
yourselves enlisted at once in our northern army. With
me it is all or nothing."

Chiao Tai's face lit up. He said eagerly, "All or
nothing, that'll be our motto!"

He rose and knelt before the magistrate, knocking
his forehead to the floor three times in succession. His
friend followed his example.

When Ma Joong and Chiao Tai had risen again
Magistrate Dee spoke.

"This is Hoong Liang, my trusted adviser, from
whom I have no secrets. You'll closely cooperate with
him. Peng-lai is my first post; I don't know how the
tribunal there is organized. But I presume that the
clerks, constables, guards and the rest of the personnel
are, as usual, locally recruited. I hear that queer things
are happening in Peng-lai, and heaven knows how far
the personnel of the tribunal is mixed up in those. I
need people by my side whom I can trust. You three

shall be my ears and eyes. Hoong, let the waiter bring a jug of wine!"

When the cups had been filled, Magistrate Dee pledged the three men in turn, and they respectfully drank to his health and his success.

The next morning when the magistrate came downstairs he found Hoong Liang and his two new assistants waiting for him in the courtyard. Ma Joong and Chiao Tai had evidently been out shopping already; they now wore neat brown robes with black sashes, small black skullcaps completing their uniforms of officers of the tribunal.

"The sky is cloudy, sir," Hoong remarked. "I fear we'll get rain."

"I strapped straw hats to the saddles," Ma Joong said. "Those should see us through to Peng-lai."

The four men mounted their horses and left the city by the east gate. For a few miles they rode along the highway crowded with travelers; then the traffic grew less. As they entered a deserted mountainous country, a horseman came galloping from the opposite direction, leading two horses on a leash. Glancing at them, Ma Joong observed, "Good horseflesh! I like that blazed one."

"The fellow shouldn't carry that box on his saddle," Chiao Tai put in. "That's asking for trouble!"

"Why?" Hoong asked.

"In these parts," Chiao Tai explained, "those red leather boxes are always used by rent collectors to carry their cash. Wise people conceal them in their saddlebags."

"The fellow seems to be in a mighty hurry," Magistrate Dee remarked casually.

At noon they reached the last mountain ridge. A torrential rain came pouring down. They took shelter under a high tree on a plateau by the roadside, overlooking the fertile green peninsula on which the district of Peng-lai was located.

While they were eating a cold snack Ma Joong told with gusto some stories about his adventures with farm girls. Magistrate Dee took no interest in ribald tales, but he had to admit that Ma Joong had a certain caustic humor that was rather amusing. But when he began on another similiar story, the magistrate cut him short saying, "I am told that there are tigers in these parts. I thought those animals favored a drier climate."

Chiao Tai, who had been listening silently to the conversation, now remarked, "Well, that's hard to say. As a rule those brutes keep to the high wooded land, but once they have acquired the taste for human flesh they'll also roam about in the plains. We might get good hunting down there!"

"What about those tales about weretigers?" Magistrate Dee asked.

Ma Joong cast an uneasy glance at the dark forest behind them.

"Never heard about it!" he said curtly.

"Could I have a look at your sword, sir?" Chiao Tai asked. "It seemed a fine antique blade to me."

As he handed him the sword, the magistrate said, "It is called Rain Dragon."

"Not the famous Rain Dragon!" Chiao Tai exclaimed ecstatically. "The blade all swordsmen under heaven talk about with awe! It was the last and best sword forged three hundred years ago by Threefinger, the greatest swordsmith that ever was!"

"Tradition has it," Magistrate Dee observed, "that Threefinger attempted to forge it eight times, but each time he failed. Then he swore he would sacrifice his beloved young wife to the river god if he were successful. The ninth time he wrought this sword. He at once beheaded his wife with it on the river bank. A fearful tempest arose and Threefinger was killed by a thunderbolt. The bodies of him and his wife were washed away by the roaring waves. This sword has been an heirloom in my family for the last two hundred years, being always passed on to the eldest son."

Chiao Tai pulled his neckcloth over his nose and mouth so as not to soil the blade with his breath. Then he drew it from the scabbard. Raising it reverently in both hands, he admired its dark-green sheen, and its hair-sharp edge that did not show a single nick. His eyes shone with a mystic fire as he spoke. "If it should be ordained that ever I should die by the sword, I pray that it may be this blade that is washed in my blood!"

With a deep bow he handed the sword back to Magistrate Dee.

The rain had changed into drizzle. They mounted their horses again and began descending the slope.

Down in the plain they saw by the roadside the stone pillar marking the boundary of the district Peng-lai. A mist hung over the muddy plain, but the magistrate still thought it a nice landscape. This was now his territory.

They rode along at a brisk pace. Late in the afternoon the city wall of Peng-lai loomed through the mist ahead.

THREE.

AN EYEWITNESS RELATES THE DISCOVERY OF A MURDER; THE JUDGE HAS A
WEIRD MEETING IN AN EMPTY HOUSE

When the four men were approaching the west gate, Chiao Tai remarked on the low walls and the modest two-storied gatehouse.

"I saw on the map," Magistrate Dee explained, "that this town has natural defenses. It is located three miles up a river, where it is joined by a broad creek. At the river mouth stands a large fort, manned by a strong garrison. They search all incoming and outgoing ships, and a few years ago, during our war with Korea, they prevented Korean war junks from entering the river. North of the river the coast consists of high cliffs, and down to the south there is nothing but swamps. Thus Peng-lai, being the only good harbor hereabouts, has become the center of our trade with Korea and Japan."

"In the capital I heard people say," Hoong added, "that many Koreans have settled down here, especially sailors, shipwrights and Buddhist monks. They live in a Korean quarter, on the other side of the creek east of the city, near where there is also a famous old Buddhist temple."

"So you can now try your luck with a Korean girl!"

Chiao Tai said to Ma Joong. "Then you can also buy off your sin cheaply in that temple!"

Two armed guards opened the gate, and they rode along a busy shopping street till they reached the high wall of the tribunal compound. They followed it till they came to the main gate, in the south wall, where a few guards were sitting on a bench under the big bronze gong.

The men sprang to their feet and saluted the magistrate sharply. But Hoong noticed that behind his back they gave each other a meaningful glance.

A constable took them to the chancery on the opposite side of the main courtyard. Four clerks were busily wielding their brushes under the supervision of a gaunt, elderly man with a short gray beard.

He came to meet them in a flurry and, stuttering, introduced himself as the senior scribe, Tang, temporarily in charge of the district administration.

"This person deeply regrets," he added nervously, "that your honor's arrival was not announced in advance. I could make no preparations for the welcome-dinner and—"

"I assumed," the magistrate interrupted him, "that the boundary post would have sent a messenger ahead. There must have been a mistake somewhere. But since I am here, you'd better show me the tribunal."

Tang first took them to the spacious court hall. The tiled floor was swept clean, and the high bench on the platform in the back was covered with a piece of shining red brocade. The entire wall behind the bench was covered with a curtain of faded violet silk. In its center appeared as usual the large figure of a unicorn, symbol of perspicacity, embroidered in thick gold thread.

They went through the door behind the curtain and, after having crossed a narrow corridor, entered the private office of the magistrate. This room was also well kept: there was not a speck of dust on the polished writing desk, the plaster walls were newly white-washed. The broad couch against the back wall was of beautiful dark green brocade. After a brief glance at the archives room next to the office, Magistrate Dee walked out into the second courtyard, which faced the reception hall. The old scribe explained nervously that the reception hall had not been used after the investigator's departure; it might be possible that a chair or a table would not be standing in its proper place. The magistrate looked curiously at the awkward, stooping figure; the man seemed very ill at ease.

"You kept everything in very good order," he said reassuringly.

Tang bowed deeply and stammered, "This person has been serving here for forty years, your honor, in fact ever since I entered the tribunal as an errand boy. I like things to be in their proper order. Everything always went so smoothly here. It is terrible that now, after all those years—"

His voice trailed off. He hurriedly opened the door of the reception hall.

When they were gathered round the high, beautifully carved center table, Tang respectfully handed the large square seal of the tribunal to the magistrate. He compared it with the impression in the register, then signed the receipt. Now he was officially in charge of the district Peng-lai.

Stroking his beard, he said, "The magistrate's murder shall take precedence over all routine affairs. In due time I'll receive the notables of the district and comply with the other formalities. Apart from the personnel of the tribunal, the only district officials I want to see today are the wardens of the four quarters of the city."

"There is a fifth here, your honor," Tang remarked. "The warden of the Korean settlement."

"Is he a Chinese?" Judge Dee asked.

"No, your honor," Tang replied, "but he speaks our language fluently." He coughed behind his hand, then went on diffidently. "I fear this is rather an unusual situation, your honor, but the prefect has decided that these Korean settlements on the east coast here shall be semiautonomous. The warden is responsible for the maintenance of the peace there; our personnel can go in only if the warden asks for their assistance."

"That's certainly an unusual situation," the judge muttered. "I'll look into that one of these days. Well, you'll now tell the entire personnel to assemble in the court hall. In the meantime, I'll just have a look at my private quarters, and refresh myself."

Tang looked embarrassed. After some hesitation he said, "Your honor's residence is in excellent condition; the late magistrate had everything painted anew last summer. Unfortunately, however, his packed-up furniture and his luggage are still standing about there. There is no news yet from his brother, his only living relative. I don't know where all those things should be sent to. And since His Excellency Wang was a widower, he had employed only local servants, who left after his . . . demise."

"Where then did the investigator stay when he came here?" the magistrate asked, astonished.

"His excellency slept on the couch in the private office, your honor," Tang answered unhappily. "The clerks also served his meals there. I deeply regret all this is highly irregular, but since the magistrate's brother does not answer my letters, I . . . It is really most unfortunate, but—"

"It doesn't matter," Judge Dee said quickly. "I hadn't planned to send for my family and servants until this murder had been solved. I'll go to my private office now and change there, and you'll show my assistants their quarters."

"Opposite the tribunal, your honor," Tang said

eagerly, "there's a very good hostel. I am staying there myself with my wife, and I can assure your honor that also his assistants—"

"That's highly irregular too," the judge interrupted coldly. "Why don't you live inside the tribunal compound? With your long experience you ought to know the rules!"

"I do have the upper floor of the building behind the reception hall, your honor," Tang explained hurriedly, "but since the roof needs repairing, I thought there would be no objection to my living, temporarily of course—"

"All right!" Judge Dee cut him short. "But I insist that my three assistants live inside. You'll have quarters arranged for them in the guardhouse."

Tang bowed deeply and left with Ma Joong and Chiao Tai. Hoong followed the judge to his private office. He helped him change into his ceremonial robe, and prepared a cup of tea for him. As the judge was rubbing his face with a hot towel he asked, "Can you imagine, Hoong, why that fellow is in such a state?"

"He seems a rather finicky kind of person," his old assistant replied. "I suppose that our unexpected arrival rather upset him."

"I rather think," Judge Dee said pensively, "that he is very much afraid of something here in the tribunal. That's also why he moved to that hostel. Well, we'll find out in due time!"

Tang came in and announced that everybody was in the court hall. Judge Dee replaced his house bonnet by the black, winged judge's cap, and went to the hall, followed by Hoong and Tang.

He took his seat behind the high bench, and motioned Ma Joong and Chiao Tai to stand behind his chair.

The judge spoke a few appropriate words, then Tang introduced to him one by one the forty men who were kneeling on the stone floor below. Judge Dee noticed that the clerks were dressed in neat blue robes, and that the leather jackets and iron helmets of the guards and constables were polished well. On the whole they seemed a decent lot. He didn't like the cruel face of the headman of the constables, but he reflected that those headmen usually were nasty fellows who needed constant supervision. The coroner, Dr. Shen, was a dignified elderly man with an intelligent face. Tang whispered to the judge that he was the best physician in the district, and a man of noble character.

When the roll call was finished, the judge announced that Hoong Liang was appointed sergeant of the tribunal and that he would control all routine affairs of the chancery. Ma Joong and Chiao Tai would supervise the constables and the guards and be responsible for the discipline, and for the guardhouse and the jail.

Back in his private office Judge Dee told Ma Joong and Chiao Tai to inspect the guardhouse and the jail. "Then," he added, "you must put the constables and the guards through a drill; that'll give you an opportunity for getting acquainted with them and to see what they are worth. Thereafter you'll go out into the town, and get an impression of things in this city. I wish I could go with you, but I'll have to devote the whole evening to getting myself orientated with regard to the magistrate's murder. Come back and report to me later in the night."

The two stalwarts left, and Tang came in followed by a clerk carrying two candlesticks. Judge Dee told Tang to sit down on the stool in front of his desk, next to Sergeant Hoong. The clerk placed the candles on the desk and noiselessly went out.

"Just now," the judge said to Tang, "I noticed that the chief clerk, listed on the roll as Fan Choong, was not there. Is he ill?"

Tang clapped his hand to his forehead. He stammered, "I had meant to speak about that, your honor. I am really greatly worried about Fan. On the first of this month he left for Pien-foo, the prefectural capital, on his yearly holiday. He was due back here yesterday morning. When he didn't appear, I sent a constable to the small farm Fan has west of the city. His tenant farmer there said Fan and his servant had arrived there yesterday, and left at noon. It's most annoying. Fan is an excellent man, a capable officer, always very punctual. I can't understand what has happened to him, he—"

"Perhaps he was devoured by a tiger," Judge Dee interrupted impatiently.

"No, your honor!" Tang cried out. "No, not that!" His face had suddenly turned ashen; the light of the candles shone in his wide, startled eyes.

"Don't be so nervous, man!" the judge said, irritated. "I quite understand that you are upset about the murder of your former chief, but that happened two weeks ago. What are you afraid of now?"

Tang wiped the sweat from his brow.

"I beg your honor's pardon," he muttered. "Last week a farmer was found in the woods, with torn throat and badly mauled. There must be a man-eater about. I am not sleeping well of late, your honor. I offer my humble excuses and—"

"Well," Judge Dee said, "my two assistants are experienced hunters; one of these days I'll send them out to kill that tiger. Get me a cup of hot tea, and let's get down to business."

When Tang had poured out a cup for the judge, he eagerly took a few sips, then settled back in his armchair.

"I want to hear from you exactly," he said, "how the murder was discovered."

Plucking at his beard, Tang began diffidently.

"Your honor's predecessor was a gentleman of considerable charm and culture. Perhaps a bit easygoing at times and impatient about details, but very precise in all things that really mattered, very precise indeed. He was about fifty years old, and he had a long and varied experience. An able magistrate, your honor."

"Did he," Judge Dee asked, "have any enemies here?"

"Not one, your honor!" Tang exclaimed. "He was a shrewd and just judge, well liked by the people. I may say, your honor, that he was popular in this district, very popular indeed."

As the judge nodded he went on.

"Two weeks ago, when the time of the morning session was approaching, his house steward came to see me in the chancery and reported that his master had not slept in his bedroom, and that the door of his library was locked on the inside. I knew that he often read and wrote in his library till deep in the night, and I presumed that he had fallen asleep over his books. So I knocked on the door insistently. When there came no sound from within, I feared that he might have had a stroke. I called the headman and had the door broken open."

Tang swallowed; his mouth twitched. After a while he went on.

"Magistrate Wang was lying on the floor in front of the tea stove, his unseeing eyes staring up at the ceiling. A teacup was lying on the mats near his outstretched right hand. I felt his body; it was stiff and cold. I immediately summoned our coroner, he stated that the magistrate must have died about midnight. He took a sample of the tea left in the teapot and—"

"Where stood that teapot?" Judge Dee interrupted.

"On the cupboard in the left corner, your honor," Tang replied, "next to the copper tea stove for boiling the water. The teapot was nearly full. Dr. Shen fed the sample to a dog, and it died at once. He heated the tea, and by the smell identified the poison. He could not test the water in the pan on the tea stove, because it had boiled dry."

"Who used to bring the tea water?" the judge asked.

"The magistrate himself," Tang answered promptly. As the judge lifted his eyebrows he explained quickly, "He was an enthusiastic devotee of the tea cult, your honor, and most particular about all its details. He always insisted on fetching the water himself from the well in his garden, and he also boiled it himself on the tea stove in his library. His teapot, cups and caddy are all valuable antiques. He kept them locked away in the cupboard under the tea stove. On my instructions the coroner also made experiments with the tea leaves found in the caddy, but those proved to be quite harmless."

"What measures did you take thereafter?" Judge Dee asked.

"I at once sent a special messenger to the prefect in Pien-foo, and I had the body placed in a temporary coffin, put up in the hall of the magistrate's private residence. Then I sealed the library. On the third day his excellency the court investigator arrived from the capital. He ordered the commander of the fort to place six secret agents of the military police at his disposal, and instituted a thorough investigation. He interrogated all the servants and he—"

"I know," Judge Dee said impatiently. "I read his report. It was clearly established that no one could have tampered with the tea, and that no one entered the library after the magistrate had retired there. When did the investigator leave exactly?"

"On the morning of the fourth day," Tang replied slowly, "the investigator summoned me and ordered me to have the coffin removed to the White Cloud Temple outside the east gate, pending the decision of the deceased's brother as to the final burying place. Then he sent the agents back to the fort, told me that he was taking all the magistrate's private papers along with him and departed." Tang looked uncomfortable. Glancing anxiously at the judge, he added, "I presume that he explained to your honor the reason for his sudden departure?"

"He said," Judge Dee improvised quickly, "that the investigation had reached a stage where it could profitably be continued by the new magistrate."

Tang seemed relieved. He asked, "I trust his excellency is in good health?"

"He has already departed for the south, on a new assignment," the judge replied. Rising, he continued. "I'll now go and have a look at the library. While I am gone you'll discuss with Sergeant Hoong what matters must be dealt with during the session tomorrow morning."

The judge took up one of the candlesticks and left.

The door of the magistrate's residence, located on the other side of a small garden behind the reception hall, was standing ajar. The rain had stopped, but a mist was hanging among the trees and over the cleverly arranged flower beds. Judge Dee pushed the door open and entered the deserted house.

He knew from the floor plan attached to the reports that the library was located at the end of the main corridor, which he found without difficulty. Walking through it he noticed two side passages, but in the limited light circle of his candle he could not see where they led to. Suddenly he halted in his steps. The light of the candle fell on a thin man who had just come out of the passage directly ahead, nearly colliding with him.

The man stood very still; he fixed the judge with a

41

queer, vacant stare. His rather regular face was disfigured by a birthmark on his left cheek, as large as a copper coin. The judge saw to his amazement that he wore no cap; his graying hair was done up in a topknot. He saw vaguely that the man was clad in a gray house robe with a black sash.

As Judge Dee opened his mouth to ask who he was, the man suddenly stepped noiselessly back into the dark passage. The judge quickly raised the candle, but the sudden movement extinguished the flame. It was pitch dark.

"Hey there, come here!" Judge Dee shouted. Only the echo answered him. He waited a moment. There was only the deep silence of the empty house.

"The impudent rascal!" Judge Dee muttered angrily. Feeling along the wall, he found his way back to the garden, and quickly went back to the office.

Tang was showing Sergeant Hoong a bulky dossier. "I want to have it understood once and for all," Judge Dee peevishly addressed Tang, "that none of the personnel shall walk about in this tribunal in undress, not even at night and when off duty. Just now I came upon a fellow wearing only a house robe, and not even a cap on his head! And the insolent yokel didn't even bother to answer me when I challenged him. Go and get him. I'll give him a good talking to!"

Tang had started to tremble all over; he looked fixedly at the judge in abject fright. Judge Dee suddenly felt sorry for him; after all, the man had been doing his best. He went on in a calmer voice. "Well, such slips will happen now and then. Who is the fellow anyway? The night watchman, I suppose?"

Tang shot a frightened look at the open door behind the judge. He stuttered, "Did ... did he wear a gray robe?"

"He did," Judge Dee replied.

"And did he have a birthmark on his left cheek?"

"He had," the judge said curtly. "But stop fidgeting, man! Speak up, who is he?"

Tang bent his head. He replied in a toneless voice, "It was the dead magistrate, your honor."

Somewhere in the compound a door slammed shut with a resounding crash.

FOUR.

JUDGE DEE GOES TO VISIT THE SCENE
OF THE CRIME; HE STUDIES THE SECRET
OF THE COPPER TEA STOVE

"What door is that?" Judge Dee barked.

"I think maybe it's the front door of the private residence, your honor," Tang replied in a faltering voice. "It doesn't shut properly."

"Have it mended tomorrow!" the judge ordered brusquely. He remained standing there, in grim silence. Slowly caressing his side whiskers, he remembered the queer vacant stare of the apparition, and how quickly and noiselessly it had disappeared.

Then he walked round his desk and sat down in his armchair. Sergeant Hoong looked at him silently, his eyes wide with horror.

With an effort Judge Dee composed himself. He studied Tang's gray face for a moment, then asked, "Have you seen that apparition too?"

Tang nodded.

"Three days ago, your honor," he replied, "and in this very office. Late at night I came here to fetch a document I needed, and he was standing there, by the side of his desk, his back turned to me."

"What happened then?" the judge asked tensely.

"I uttered a cry, your honor, and let the candle drop. I ran outside and called the guards. When we came back, the room was empty." Tang passed his hand over

44

his eyes, then added, "He looked exactly as we found him, your honor, that morning in his library. Then he was wearing his gray house robe with the black sash. His cap had dropped from his head when he fell on the floor . . . dead."

As Judge Dee and Sergeant Hoong remained silent, he went on.

"I am convinced that the investigator must have seen him too, your honor! That is why he looked so ill that last morning, and why he left so abruptly."

The judge tugged at his mustache. After a while he said gravely, "It would be foolish to deny the existence of supernatural phenomena. We must never forget that our Master Confucius himself was very noncommittal when his disciples questioned him on those things. On the other hand, I am inclined to begin by seeking for a rational explanation."

Hoong slowly shook his head.

"There's none, your honor," he remarked. "The only explanation is that the dead magistrate can't find rest because his murder is not yet avenged. His body is lying in the Buddhist temple, and they say that it is easy for a dead man to manifest himself to the living in the proximity of his corpse, and when decomposition has not yet advanced too far."

Judge Dee rose abruptly.

"I shall give this problem serious thought," he said. "Now I'll go back to the house and examine the library."

"You can't risk meeting the ghost again, sir!" Sergeant Hoong exclaimed, aghast.

"Why not?" Judge Dee asked. "The dead man's purpose is to have his murder avenged. He must know that I have the same desire. Why then should he want to harm me? When you are through here, sergeant, come and join me in the library. You can take two guards with lampions along if you want."

Ignoring their protests, Judge Dee left the office. This time he first walked over to the chancery and fetched there a large lantern of oiled paper.

When he was again in the deserted house he entered the side passage where the apparition had disappeared. On either side was a door. Opening the one on his right he saw a spacious room, the floor covered with larger and smaller bundles and boxes, piled up in confusion. Placing the lantern on the floor, Judge Dee felt the bundles and looked among the piled-up boxes. A grotesque shadow in the corner startled him. Then he realized it was his own. There was nothing there but the belongings of the dead man.

Shaking his head, the judge entered the room opposite. It was empty but for a few large pieces of furniture, packed up in straw mats.

The passage ended in a massive door, securely locked and bolted. Deep in thought the judge walked back to the corridor.

The door at its end was elaborately carved with motifs of clouds and dragons, but its beauty was marred by a few boards nailed over the upper part. There the constables had smashed the panel in order to open the door.

Judge Dee tore off the strip of paper with the seal of the tribunal, and opened the door. Holding his lantern high he surveyed the small, square room, simply but elegantly furnished. On the left was a high, narrow window; directly in front of it stood a heavy ebony cupboard, bearing a large copper tea stove. On the stove stood a round pewter pan for boiling the tea water. Next to the stove he saw a small teapot of exquisite blue and white porcelain. The rest of the wall was taken up entirely by bookshelves, as was the wall opposite. The back wall had a low, broad window; its paper panes were scrupulously clean. In front of the window stood an antique desk of rosewood, with three drawers on either end, and a comfortable armchair, also of rosewood, covered with a red satin cushion. The desk was empty but for two copper candlesticks.

The judge stepped inside and examined the dark stain on the reed mats, between the tea cupboard and the desk. Presumably that stain was caused by the tea spilling from the magistrate's cup when he fell down. Probably he had put the water on the fire, then had sat down at his desk. When he had heard the water boil, he had gone to the tea stove and poured the water into the teapot. Standing there he had filled his cup, and taken a sip from it. Then the poison had taken its effect.

Seeing a key stuck in the elaborate lock of the cupboard, the judge opened it and looked with admiration at the choice collection of utensils of the tea cult that were stacked on the two shelves. There was not a speck of dust; evidently the investigator and his assistants had been over everything very thoroughly.

He walked over to the desk. The drawers were empty. There the investigator had found the dead man's private papers. The judge heaved a deep sigh. It was a great pity that he had not seen the room directly after the murder had been discovered.

Turning to the shelves, he ran his finger idly over the tops of the books. They were covered with a thick layer of dust. Judge Dee smiled contentedly. Here was at least something new to examine; the investigator and his men had apparently ignored the books. Surveying the packed shelves, the judge decided to wait with his examination till Hoong would have come.

He turned the armchair round so that it faced the door, then sat down. Folding his arms in his wide sleeves, he tried to imagine what kind of man the murderer could have been. To kill an imperial official is a crime against the state, for which the law prescribes the death penalty in one of its most severe forms, such as the hideous "lingering death" or being quartered alive. The murderer must have had a very strong motive indeed. And how had he poisoned the tea? It had to be the tea water in the pan, for the unused tea leaves had been tested and found harmless. The only other solution he could think of was that the murderer had sent or given the magistrate a small quantity of tea leaves, just enough for making tea once, and that those had contained the poison.

Judge Dee sighed again. He thought of the apparition he had seen. It was the first time in his life he had actually seen such a ghostly phenomenon and he still wasn't quite convinced that it had been real. It could have been a hoax of some kind. But then the investigator and Tang had also seen it. Who would dare to take the risk to pose as a ghost, inside the tribunal itself? And for what reason? He thought that after all it must indeed have been the ghost of the dead magistrate. Reclining his head on the back rest, the judge closed his eyes and tried to visualize the face of the apparition as he had seen it. Was it not possible that the dead man would give him some token to assist him in solving the riddle?

He quickly opened his eyes, but the room was as still and empty as before. The judge remained a few moments as he was, idly surveying the red-lacquered ceiling, crossed by four heavy roof beams. He noticed a discolored spot on the ceiling and a few dusty cobwebs in the corner where the tea cupboard stood. Evidently the dead magistrate had not been as fussy about cleanliness as his senior scribe.

Then Sergeant Hoong came in, followed by two guards carrying large candlesticks. Judge Dee ordered them to place the candles on the desk, then dismissed them.

"The only things left for us here, sergeant," he said, "are those books and document rolls on the shelves.

It's quite a lot, but if you hand me a pile and replace it when I am through, it shouldn't take too long!"

Hoong nodded cheerfully and took a pile of books from the nearest shelf. As he rubbed off the dust with his sleeve, the judge turned his chair round again so that it faced the desk, and he started to look through the books the sergeant put in front of him.

More than two hours had passed when Hoong replaced the last pile on the shelves. Judge Dee leaned back in his chair and took a folding fan from his sleeve. Fanning himself vigorously, he said with a contented smile, "Well, Hoong, I have now a fairly clear picture of the murdered man's personality. I have glanced through the volumes with his own poetry; it is written in exquisite style but rather shallow in content. Love poems predominate, most of them dedicated to famous courtesans in the capital or other places where Magistrate Wang served."

"Tang made some veiled remarks just now, your honor," Hoong put in, "to the effect that the magistrate was a man of rather slack morals. He often even invited prostitutes to his house, and had them stay there overnight."

Judge Dee nodded.

"That brocade folder you gave me a few moments ago," he said, "contained nothing but erotic drawings. Further, he had a few score books on wine, and the way it is made in various parts of the empire, and on cooking. On the other hand, he had built up a fine collection of the great ancient poets, every volume dogeared and with his own notes and comments written in on nearly every page. The same goes for his comprehensive collection of works on Buddhism and on Taoist mysticism. But his edition of the complete Confucian classics is in as virginal a state as when he purchased it! I further noticed that the sciences are well represented: most of the standard works on medicine

49

and alchemy are there, also a few rare old treatises on riddles, conundrums and mechanical devices. Books on history, statecraft, administration and mathematics are conspicuous by their absence."

Turning his chair round, the judge continued.

"I conclude that Magistrate Wang was a poet with a keen sense of beauty, and also a philosopher deeply interested in mysticism. And at the same time he was a sensual man, much attached to all earthly pleasures—a not unusual combination, I believe. He was completely devoid of ambition; he liked the post of magistrate in a quiet district far from the capital, where he was his own master and where he could arrange his life as he liked. That is why he didn't want to be promoted—I believe that Peng-lai was already his ninth post as magistrate! But he was a very intelligent man of an inquisitive mind—hence his interest in riddles, conundrums and mechanical devices—and that, together with his long practical experience, made him a fairly satisfactory magistrate here, although I don't suppose he was very devoted to his duties. He cared little for family ties; that is why he didn't remarry after his first and second ladies had died, and why he was content with ephemeral liaisons with courtesans and prostitutes. He himself summed up his own personality rather aptly in the name he bestowed on his library."

Judge Dee pointed with his fan at the inscribed board that hung over the door. Hoong couldn't help smiling when he read, "Hermitage of the Vagrant Weed."

"However," the judge resumed, "I found one very striking inconsistency." Tapping the oblong notebook that he had kept apart, he asked, "Where did you find this, sergeant?"

"It had fallen behind the books on this lower shelf," Hoong replied, pointing.

"In this notebook," Judge Dee said, "the magistrate copied out with his own hand long lists of dates and figures, and added pages of complicated calculations. There is not one word of explanation. But Mr. Wang seems to me the last man to be interested in figures. I suppose he left all financial and statistical work to Tang and the clerks, didn't he?"

Sergeant Hoong nodded emphatically.

"So Tang gave me to understand just now," he replied.

Judge Dee leafed through the notebook, slowly shaking his head. He said pensively, "He spent an enormous amount of time and labor on these notes—small mistakes are carefully blotted out and corrected, etc. The only clue is the dates, the earliest mentioned is exactly two months ago."

He rose and put the notebook in his sleeve.

"In any case," he said, "I'll study this at leisure, though it is of course by no means certain that it concerns affairs that are connected with his murder. But inconsistencies are always worth special attention. Anyway we have now a good picture of the victim, and that's, according to our handbooks on detection, the first step toward discovering the murderer!"

FIVE.

TWO STALWARTS HAVE A GRATIS MEAL IN A RESTAURANT; THEY WATCH A STRANGE PERFORMANCE ON THE WATER FRONT

"The first thing to do," Ma Joong said when he left the tribunal together with Chiao Tai, "is to get something under our belts. Drilling those lazy bastards made me hungry."

"And thirsty!" Chiao Tai added.

They entered the first restaurant they saw, a small place on the corner southwest of the tribunal. It bore the lofty name of Nine Flowers Orchard. They were met by the din of confused voices; it was very crowded. They found with difficulty an empty place near the high counter in the back, behind which a one-armed man stood stirring an enormous kettle of noodles.

The two friends surveyed the crowd. They were mostly small shopkeepers, taking a quick snack before they would have to hurry back to meet the evening rush of customers. They were gobbling their noodles with relish, stopping only to pass the pewter wine jugs around.

Chiao Tai grabbed the waiter's sleeve when he hurried past them with a tray loaded with noodle bowls.

"Four of those!" he said. "And two large jugs!"

"Later!" the waiter snapped. "Can't you see I am busy?"

Chiao Tai burst out in a string of picturesque curses. The one-armed man looked up and stared intently at him. He laid down the long bamboo ladle and came round the counter, his sweat-covered face creased in a broad grin.

"There was but one over there who could curse like that!" he exclaimed. "What brought you here, sir?"

"Forget the sir," Chiao Tai said gruffly. "I got into trouble when we were moved up north, and gave up my rank and my name. I am called Chiao Tai now. Can't you get us a bit of food?"

"One moment, sir," the man said eagerly. He disappeared into the kitchen, and presently came back followed by a fat woman, who carried a tray with two large wine jugs and a platter heaped with salted fish and vegetables.

"That's better!" Chiao Tai said contentedly. "Sit down, soldier, let your old woman do the work for once!"

The owner drew up a stool, and his wife took his place behind the counter. While the two friends started eating and drinking, the owner told them that he was a native of Peng-lai. After he had been discharged from the expeditionary force in Korea, he had bought the restaurant with his savings and wasn't doing too badly. Looking at the brown robes of the two men, he asked in a low voice, "Why do you work in that tribunal?"

"For the same reason you are stirring noodles," Chiao Tai replied. "To earn a living."

The one-armed man looked left and right. Then he whispered, "Queer things are happening there! Don't you know that a fortnight ago they throttled the magistrate and chopped up his body into small pieces?"

"I thought he was poisoned!" Ma Joong remarked, taking a long draught from his wine cup.

"That's what they say!" the owner said. "A kettle of mincemeat, that was all that was left of that magistrate! Believe me, the people there are no good."

"The present magistrate is a fine fellow," Chiao Tai remarked.

"I don't know about him," the man said stubbornly, "but Tang and Fan, those two are no good."

"What's wrong with the old dodderer?" Chiao Tai asked, astonished. "He looks to me as if he couldn't hurt a fly."

"Leave him alone!" the owner said darkly. "He is ... different, you know. Besides, there's something else very wrong with Tang."

"What something?" Ma Joong asked.

"There's more happening in this district than meets the eye, I tell you," the one-armed man said. "I am a native, I should know! Since olden times there have been some weird people here. My old father used to tell us stories—"

His voice trailed off. He shook his head sadly, then quickly emptied the wine cup which Chiao Tai pushed over to him.

Ma Joong shrugged his shoulders.

"We'll find out for ourselves," he remarked, "that's half of the fun. As to that fellow Fan you mentioned, we'll worry about him afterward. The guards told me he's kind of lost, just now."

"I hope he'll stay that way!" the one-armed man said with feeling. "That bully takes money from all and sundry, he is even more greedy than the headman there. And what's worse, he can't leave the women alone. He is a good-looking rascal, heaven knows what mischief he has made already! But he is thick as thieves with Tang, and that fellow always manages to shield him."

"Well," Chiao Tai put in, "Fan's palmy days are over; he'll have to work under me and my friend here now. He must have collected plenty of bribes though. I hear he owns a small farm west of the city."

"That he inherited last year from a distant relative," the owner said. "It isn't much good, it's a lonely small place, and near the deserted temple. Well, if it's there he got lost, it's they who must have got him."

"Can't you talk plain Chinese for once?" Ma Joong exclaimed impatiently. "Who is 'they'?"

The one-armed man shouted to the waiter. When he had placed two enormous bowls with noodles on the table, the owner spoke, softly.

"To the west of Fan's farm, where the country road joins the highway, there stands an old temple. Nine years ago four monks lived there; they belonged to the White Cloud Temple, outside the east gate. One morning all four were found dead, their throats slit from ear to ear! They were not replaced, the temple has been standing empty ever since. But the ghosts of those four men are still haunting the place. Farmers have seen lights there at night. and everybody gives it a wide berth. Only last week a cousin of mine who passed by there late in the night saw in the moonlight a headless monk slinking about. He saw clearly that he was carrying his severed head under his arm."

"August heaven!" Chiao Tai shouted. "Stop those tales of horror, will you? How can I eat my noodles when they are standing on end in the bowl?"

Ma Joong guffawed. They started on the noodles in earnest. When they had finished their bowls to the last drop. Chiao Tai rose and groped in his sleeve. The owner quickly put his hand on his arm and exclaimed, "Never, sir! This restaurant and all in it is yours. If it hadn't been for you, those Korean lancers would—"

"All right!" Chiao Tai interrupted him. "Thanks for your hospitality. But if you want to see us back here, next time we'll pay cash!"

The one-armed man protested energetically, but Chiao Tai clapped his shoulder and they left.

Outside Chiao Tai said to Ma Joong, "Now that

we have eaten our fill, brother, we had better do some work! Now how does one get an impression of a town?"

Ma Joong looked at the thick fog. Scratching his head, he replied. "I suppose it's done by sheer foot-work, brother!"

They walked along, keeping close to the lighted shop fronts. Despite the mist there were a good many people about. The two friends looked idly at the local goods on display, and here and there inquired about prices. Arrived at the gate of the Temple of the War God, they went inside, bought for a few coppers a bunch of incense sticks and burned them before the altar, praying for the souls of the soldiers fallen in battle.

When they were strolling south again, Ma Joong asked, "Do you know why we are all the time fighting beyond our frontiers against those barbarians there? Why not let the bastards stew in their own grease?"

"You don't know a thing about politics, brother," Chiao Tai replied condescendingly. "It is our duty to deliver them from their barbarism, and to teach them our culture!"

"Well," Ma Joong remarked, "those Tartars also know a thing or two. Do you know why they don't insist on their girls being virgins when they are married? Because, my friend, they make allowances for the fact that those Tartar girls, from childhood, are always riding on horseback! But don't let our own girls come to know about that!"

"I wish you would stop your prattle!" Chiao Tai exclaimed, irritated. "Now we have lost our way."

They found themselves in what seemed to be a residential quarter. The street was paved with smooth flagstones, and on either side they vaguely saw the high walls of large mansions. It was very still, the mist deadened all sound.

"That there in front of us is a bridge, isn't it?" Ma Joong said. "That must be the canal that crosses the southern half of the city. If we just follow that canal in an easterly direction, we'll probably get to a shopping street again, sooner or later."

They crossed the bridge, and started to walk along the waterside.

Suddenly Ma Joong laid his hand on Chiao Tai's arm. He pointed silently to the opposite bank, faintly visible through the mist.

Chiao Tai strained his eyes. A group of men seemed to be moving along there, carrying on their shoulders a small, open litter. In the gray moonlight that filtered through the mist he saw on the litter the figure of a bareheaded man, sitting cross-legged with his arms folded on his breast. He seemed all swathed up in white.

"Who's that queer fellow?" Chiao Tai asked, amazed.

"Heaven knows," Ma Joong growled. "Look, they are halting."

A gust of wind blew a wisp of mist away. They saw that the men had put the litter down. Suddenly two men standing behind the seated man lifted large clubs, and let them descend on his head and shoulders. Then the mist thickened again. They heard a splash.

Ma Joong cursed.

"To the bridge!" he hissed at Chiao Tai.

They turned round and ran back along the canal. But they couldn't see well, and the ground was slippery; it took them quite some time to get back to the bridge. They quickly crossed it, then cautiously made their way along the opposite bank. But everything seemed deserted. After they had walked up and down for some time along the stretch where they thought they had seen the attack, Ma Joong suddenly stooped and felt the ground with his fingers.

"There are deep marks here," he said. "This must

be the place where they dumped the poor bastard into the canal."

The mist was lifting a little now, they could see a patch of muddy water several feet below them. Ma Joong stripped naked. Having given his robes to Chiao Tai he stepped out of his boots and lowered himself into the water. It came up to his midriff.

"It stinks!" he remarked sourly. "But I see no dead body."

He waded out further. When he came back to the bank he felt with his feet in the thick layer of dirt and mud on the bottom of the canal.

"Nothing doing," he muttered disgustedly. "We must have mistaken the place. There's nothing here but a few large lumps of clay or stone, and caked waste paper. What a mess! Pull me up."

It started raining.

"That's the only thing we were lacking!" Chiao Tai said with a curse. Noticing that there was a porch over the back door of the dark, silent mansion behind him, Chiao Tai took shelter there with Ma Joong's clothes and boots. Ma Joong remained standing in the rain till it had washed his body clean again. Then he joined Chiao Tai under the porch and rubbed himself dry with his neckcloth. When the rain had stopped, they set out again in an easterly direction, along the canal. The mist had grown thinner. They saw on their left a long row of the high back walls of large houses.

"We didn't do too well, brother," Chiao Tai said ruefully. "More experienced officers would doubtless have got those fellows."

"Even experienced officers can't fly over a canal!" Ma Joong replied sourly. "What a weird sight was that swathed-up fellow. And that right on top of those cheerful tales your one-armed friend had been telling. Let's find a place where we can have another drink."

They walked on till they saw the blurred light of a

colored lantern through the dripping mist. It marked the side entrance of a large restaurant. They went round to the front. Entering the beautifully furnished waiting room downstairs, they scowled at a supercilious waiter who looked critically at their wet robes, and went up the broad staircase. As they pushed open the elaborately carved double doors they saw a spacious dining room, alive with the hubbub of voices.

SIX.

A DRUNKEN POET COMPOSES A SONG TO THE MOON; CHIAO TAI MEETS A KOREAN GIRL IN A BROTHEL

Looking at the neatly-dressed, sedate people who were crowding round the marble-topped tables, the two friends reflected that this restaurant was far above their financial status.

"Let's go somewhere else." Ma Joong muttered.

As he turned round to go, a thin man who was sitting alone at a table near the door rose from his chair. He said in a thick voice, "Sit down and join me, my friends! Drinking alone always saddens me."

He looked at them with watery eyes from under queerly shaped, arched eyebrows that gave him a perpetual questioning look. They noticed that he wore a dark blue robe of costly silk, and a high cap of black velvet. But there were stains on his collar, and untidy locks of hair came out from under his cap. He had a bloated face, and a thin, long nose with a shining red tip.

"Since he asks for it, let's keep him company a bit," Chiao Tai said. "I wouldn't like that yokel downstairs to think that we had been kicked out!"

The two friends sat down opposite their host, who immediately ordered two large jugs of wine.

"What might you be doing for a living?" Ma Joong asked when the waiter had gone.

"I am Po Kai, the business manager of the ship-owner Yee Pen," the thin man replied. He emptied his cup in one draught, then added proudly, "But I am also a well-known poet."

"Since you pay for the drinks, we won't hold that against you," Ma Joong said generously.

He lifted the wine jug, threw his head back and slowly let half of its contents pour down his throat. Chiao Tai followed his example. Po Kai watched this performance eagerly.

"Neat!" he said with approval. "In this particular establishment one as a rule uses a cup, but I think your method is of refreshing simplicity."

"It just so happens that we are in need of a long drink," Ma Joong said as he wiped his mouth with a sigh of satisfaction.

Po Kai refilled his own cup, then said, "Tell me a good story! You fellows who live by the road must lead an eventful life."

"Live by the road?" Ma Joong exclaimed indignantly. "Look here, my man, you'd better mind your language. We are officers of the tribunal!"

Po Kai lifted his arched eyebrows still higher. He shouted at the waiter, "Bring another wine jug, the largest!" Then he went on. "Well well, so you two are the men the new magistrate imported here today. But he must have recruited you only recently, for you haven't yet got that smug look of petty officials."

"Did you know the former magistrate?" Chiao Tai asked. "They say he also was some sort of poet."

"Hardly," Po Kai replied. "I am rather new here, you know." He suddenly put down his cup and exclaimed happily, "That was the last line I was trying

61

to think of!" Looking solemnly at the two friends, he added, "This line completes a great poem dedicated to the moon. Shall I recite it for you?"

"No!" Ma Joong said, horrified.

"Shall I sing it then?" Po Kai asked hopefully. "I have a rather good voice, you know, and the other guests here would greatly appreciate it."

"No!" Ma Joong and Chiao Tai answered at the same time. Seeing the other's hurt look, Chiao Tai added, "We just don't like poetry, in any shape or form."

"That's a pity!" Po Kai remarked. "Are you two perhaps students of Buddhism?"

"Is the fellow trying to pick a quarrel?" Ma Joong asked Chiao Tai suspiciously.

"He is drunk," Chiao Tai answered indifferently. And to Po Kai, "Don't tell me that you are a Buddhist!"

"A devout devotee," Po Kai replied primly. "I regularly visit the White Cloud Temple. The abbot is a holy man, and the Prior Hui-pen delivers the most beautiful sermons. The other day—"

"Listen," Chiao Tai interrupted, "shall we have another drink?"

Po Kai gave him a reproachful look. He rose with a deep sigh and said resignedly, "Let's have it with the wenches."

"Now you are talking!" Ma Joong said with enthusiasm. "Do you know a good place?"

"Does the horse know its stable?" Po Kai asked with a sniff. He paid the bill and they left.

A heavy fog still hung in the street. Po Kai took them to the waterside at the back of the restaurant, and whistled on his fingers. The bow lantern of a small barge emerged from the mist.

Po Kai stepped inside and said to the rower, "To the boat."

"Hey!" Ma Joong shouted. "Didn't I hear you speak about the wenches?"

"Same thing, same thing!" Po Kai replied airily. "Step inside." To the boatman he added, "Take the short cut, the gentlemen are in a great hurry."

He crawled under the low roofmat, and Ma Joong and Chiao Tai squatted down by his side. They glided along through the mist; the splashing of the oar was the only sound they heard.

After a time the sound ceased; the boat went on silently. The boatman extinguished the lantern. The boat lay still.

Ma Joong laid his heavy hand on Po Kai's shoulder. "If this is a trap," he said casually, "I'll break your neck."

"Don't talk nonsense!" Po Kai exclaimed testily.

There was the clanking of iron, then the boat moved on again.

"We passed under the east watergate," Po Kai explained. "Part of the trellis is loose. But don't tell that to your boss!"

Soon the black hulls of a row of large barges rose up in front of them.

"The second, as usual," Po Kai ordered the boatman.

When their boat was alongside the gangway, Po Kai gave the man a few coppers and climbed on board, followed by Ma Joong and Chiao Tai.

He picked his way through a number of small tables and footstools that were standing about in confusion on the deck, and knocked on the door of the cabin. A fat woman dressed in a soiled black silk gown opened. She grinned, showing a row of black teeth.

"Welcome back, Mr. Po Kai!" she said. "Please come downstairs."

They descended a steep wooden ladder, and found

themselves in a large cabin, dimly lighted by two colored lampions hanging from the roof beam.

The three men sat down at the large table that took up most of the room space. The fat woman clapped her hands. A squat man with a coarse face came in, carrying a tray with wine jugs.

As he poured out the drinks Po Kai asked the woman, "Where is my good friend and colleague Kim Sang?"

"He hasn't come yet," she replied. "But I'll see to it that you won't get bored!"

She gave a sign to the waiter. He opened the door in the back, and four girls came in, dressed only in thin summer robes. Po Kai greeted them boisterously.

Dragging down one girl on either side of him, he said, "I'll take these two! Not for what you think," he added quickly to Ma Joong and Chiao Tai, "but only to make absolutely sure that my cup is never empty."

Ma Joong motioned a plump girl with a pleasant round face to his side, and Chiao Tai started a conversation with the fourth. He thought she was very good-looking but she seemed in a morose mood and answered only when spoken to. Her name was Yü-soo, she was a Korean, but spoke very good Chinese.

"Yours is a beautiful country," Chia Tai remarked as he put his arm around her waist. "I was there during the war."

The girl pushed him away and gave him a contemptuous look.

He realized that he had made a bad mistake and said hurriedly, "Your people are excellent fighters, they did what they could, but they were outnumbered by our troops."

The girl ignored him.

64

"Can't you smile and talk, wench?" the fat woman snapped at her.

"Leave me alone, will you?" the girl said slowly to her. "The customer doesn't complain, does he?"

The woman got up. Raising her hand to slap Yü-soo, she hissed, "I'll teach you manners, you slut!"

Chiao Tai pushed her back roughly. He growled, "Keep your hands off the girl."

"Let's go up on deck!" Po Kai shouted. "I feel in my liver that the moon is out! Kim Sang will be here soon."

"I'll stay here," the Korean girl told Chiao Tai.

"As you like," he said, and followed the others up on deck.

A bleak moon shone on the row of barges moored along the city wall. Over the dark water of the creek they vaguely saw the opposite bank.

Ma Joong sat down on a low stool and took the plump girl on his lap. Po Kai pushed his two friends over to Chiao Tai.

"Keep them happy," he said. "My mind is now on higher things."

He remained standing, his hands on his back, looking up ecstatically at the moon.

Suddenly he said, "Since all of you keep insisting, I shall now sing for you my new poem."

Stretching out his scraggy neck, he burst out in a piercing falsetto voice.

> Peerless companion of song and dance,
> Friend of the gay, comforter of the sad,
> Oh moon, oh silvery moon—

He paused for breath, then suddenly lowered his head, listening. Giving the others a quick look, he said peevishly, "I hear an unpleasant noise!"

65

"So do I!" Ma Joong remarked. "Holy heaven, don't make those awful sounds. Can't you see I am talking seriously with this wench?"

"I was referring to the sounds from below," Po Kai replied stiffly. "I presume that your friend's friend is receiving a gentle correction."

As he fell silent they heard from below the sound of blows and muffled groans. Chiao Tai jumped up and rushed down, with Ma Joong on his heels.

The Korean girl had been stripped naked and laid across the table. The waiter was holding her hands, another man her legs. The fat woman was beating her across her hips with a rattan stick.

Chiao Tai knocked the waiter down with a hard blow on his jaw. The other man let go of the girl's legs and drew a knife from his girdle.

Chiao Tai vaulted over the table, threw the woman with her back against the wall, caught the knife-wielder's wrist and gave it a quick twist. The man fell back with a yell of pain; the knife clattered to the floor.

The girl let herself roll from the table, tearing frantically at the dirty rag with which she had been gagged. Chiao Tai helped her up and freed her of the gag.

The other man stooped to pick up the knife with his left hand, but Ma Joong gave him a kick in his ribs that sent him doubled up into a corner. The girl was retching violently; suddenly she started to vomit.

"One happy little family!" Po Kai remarked from the stairs.

"Call the men from the next boat!" the fat woman panted at the waiter, who was scrambling up.

"Call all the bastards together!" Ma Joong shouted with enthusiasm. He broke a leg from his chair to be used as a club.

"Slowly, auntie, slowly!" Po Kai called out. "Better be careful. These two men are officers of the tribunal."

The woman grew pale. She quickly motioned the waiter to come back.

Falling on her knees before Chiao, she whined, "Please, sir, I only wanted to teach her how to behave to you!"

"I told you to keep your dirty hands off her!" Chiao Tai snapped. He gave the girl his neckcloth to clean her face. She rose and stood there trembling.

"Go and comfort her a bit, brother," Ma Joong counseled. "I'll put that fellow with the knife on his feet again."

Yü-soo took up her robe and went to the door in the back. Chiao Tai followed her into a narrow corridor. The girl opened one of the doors that lined it and motioned Chiao Tai to go inside. Then she went on.

Chiao Tai saw that the cabin was very small. A bed stood under the porthole, the only other furniture was a small dressing table with a rickety bamboo taboret in front of it, and a large red leather clothes box against the wall opposite.

Chiao Tai sat down on the clothes box and waited till Yü-soo came in.

As she silently threw her robe on the bed Chiao Tai said awkwardly, "I am sorry, it was all my fault."

"It doesn't matter," the girl said indifferently. She bent over the bed and took a small round box from the windowsill. Chiao Tai could not take his eyes off her shapely figure.

"Better get dressed," he said gruffly.

"It's too hot in here," Yü-soo said in a sullen voice. She had opened the box and was rubbing ointment on the welts across her hips.

"Look," she said suddenly, "you were just in time! The skin is not yet broken."

"Won't you please put that dress on?" Chiao Tai said hoarsely.

"I thought you'd be interested to know," the girl said placidly. "You said yourself it was your fault, didn't you?" She folded her robe up, placed it on the taboret. She sat down carefully and started to do up her hair.

Chiao Tai looked at her well-formed back. He told himself angrily that it would be mean to bother her now. Then he saw her firm round breasts reflected in the mirror.

He swallowed and said desperately, "Don't do that! Two of you is just too much for any man."

Yü-soo looked round at him, astonished. Then she shrugged her shapely shoulders, rose and sat down on the bed opposite Chiao Tai.

"Are you really from the tribunal?" she asked casually. "People here often tell lies, you know."

Grateful for the diversion Chiao Tai pulled a folded document from his boot. The girl wiped her hands off on her hair, then took it.

"I can't read," she remarked, "but I have good eyes!"

Turning over on her belly, she reached down behind the bed and brought out a flat, square package, tightly wrapped in gray paper. Sitting up again, she compared the seal on Chiao Tai's pass with that impressed over the folds of the wrapper.

Handing the pass back to him, she said, "You are right. It's the same seal."

She looked pensively at Chiao Tai, slowly scratching her thigh.

"How did you get that package with the seal of the tribunal?" Chiao Tai asked curiously.

"Look, he has come to life," the girl said, pouting. "You are a real thief catcher, aren't you?"

Chiao Tai clenched his fists.

"Look here, woman!" he blurted out. "You just got

hurt, didn't you? You don't think that I would be so mean as to want to sleep with you now, do you?"

The girl gave him a sidelong glance. She yawned, then said slowly, "I am not so sure I'd think that mean of you."

Chiao Tai quickly got up.

When he came back in the main cabin he found Po Kai sitting at the table, his head cradled in his arms. He was snoring loudly. The fat woman sat opposite him, looking morosely at a cup of wine. Chiao Tai settled the bill with her, and warned her that she would get into serious trouble with him if she maltreated the Korean girl again.

"She's only a Korean war slave, sir, and I bought her from the government in the regular way," she said sharply. Then she added ingratiatingly, "But your word is of course law to me, sir."

Ma Joong came in, looking very pleased.

"After all, this is rather a cosy place," he remarked. "And that plump girl is first class!"

"I hope soon to have something better for you, sir!" the woman said eagerly. "There's a brand-new one on the fifth boat, a real beauty and well educated too. Just now she is being kept reserved for a certain gentleman but, well, those things don't last forever, as you know! Maybe in a week or two—"

"Splendid!" exclaimed Ma Joong. "We'll be back. But tell those men of yours not to wave knives at us. That upsets us, and when we are upset we are liable to become a bit rough." Shaking Po Kai's shoulder he shouted in his ear, "Wake up, gay songster! It's nearly midnight, time to go home!"

Po Kai raised his head. He gave the two men a jaundiced look.

"You two are utterly vulgar," he remarked haughtily. "You'll never understand my lofty spirit. I prefer to wait here for my good friend Kim Sang. Your company is distasteful to me, you think only of drinking and fornication. Go away; I despise you!"

Ma Joong roared with laughter. He pushed Po Kai's cap down over his eyes, then he went up with Chiao Tai and whistled for a boat.

SEVEN.

JUDGE DEE HEARS THE REPORT ON THE LACQUER BOX; HE GOES TO VISIT A TEMPLE IN THE DEAD OF NIGHT

When Ma Joong and Chiao Tai came back to the tribunal they saw a light in Judge Dee's private office. They found him closeted there with Sergeant Hoong. His desk was piled with dossiers and document rolls.

The judge motioned them to sit down on the stools in front of the desk, then said, "Tonight I examined together with Hoong the magistrate's library, but we couldn't discover how the tea had been poisoned. Since the tea stove stands in front of a window, Hoong thought that perhaps the murderer had pushed a thin blowpipe through the paper window pane from outside, and had thus blown the poison powder into the pan with tea water. But when we went back to the library to verify this theory, we found that outside the window there are heavy shutters, which haven't been opened for months. That window gives onto a dark corner of the garden; therefore the dead magistrate used only the other window, in front of his writing desk.

"Just before dinner I received the four city wardens. They seemed rather decent fellows to me. The warden of the Korean settlement came also, a capable man. It seems that in his own country he is an official of some sort." The judge paused a while, glancing through the notes he had been making while talking with Hoong.

71

"After dinner," he resumed, "I went over with Hoong the most important files in the archives here, and found that all the registers are kept carefully up to date." He pushed the file in front of him away, and asked briskly, "Well, how did it fare with you two tonight?"

"I fear we didn't do too well, magistrate," Ma Joong said ruefully. "Me and my friend will have to learn this job from the bottom up, so to speak."

"I have to learn it myself, too," Judge Dee remarked with a wan smile. "What happened?"

First Ma Joong reported what the owner of the Nine Flowers Orchard had told them about Tang and his assistant, Fan Choong. When he had finished Judge Dee said, shaking his head, "I don't understand what is wrong with that fellow Tang; the man is in a terrible state. He imagines he has seen the ghost of the dead magistrate, and that seems to have shocked him deeply. But I suspect there's something else, too. The man got on my nerves. I sent him home after I had taken my after-dinner tea.

"As to Fan Choong, we shouldn't attach too much value to what that innkeeper said. Those people are often prejudiced against the tribunal; they don't like our controlling the rice price, the enforcement of the taxes on liquor and so on. We'll form our own opinion of him when he has turned up again."

The judge took a few sips from his tea, then resumed.

"By the way, Tang told me that there's really a man-eating tiger about here. A week ago he killed a farmer. As soon as we have made some progress with the murder investigation, you two might have a try at getting that brute."

"That's a job we like, magistrate!" Ma Joong said eagerly. Then his face fell. After some hesitation he told about the murderous attack they thought they had witnessed on the bank of the canal.

Judge Dee looked worried. Pursing his lips, he said, "Let's hope the mist played you a trick. I wouldn't like to have a second murder on my hands just now! Go back there tomorrow morning and see whether you can't find out more from the people living in that neighborhood. Perhaps there is a quite normal explanation for what you saw. And we'll see whether someone is reported missing."

Then Chiao Tai reported on their meeting with Yee Pen's manager, Po Kai, and gave a chastened version of their visit to the floating brothels. He said they had drunk a cup of wine there, and talked a bit with the girls.

To their relief the two friends saw that the judge seemed pleased with their reports.

"You didn't do badly at all!" he said. "You have gathered much information, and brothels are the meeting place of all the riff-raff of a town. It is good that you know your way about there now. Let's see where exactly those boats are located. Sergeant, give me that map we were looking at."

Hoong unrolled a pictorial map of the city on the desk. Ma Joong rose and, bending over it, he pointed at the second bridge over the canal, east of the watergate in the southwest quarter.

"Somewhere near here," he said, "we saw that man in the litter. Then we met Po Kai in the restaurant here, and went by boat east, along the canal. We left by the other watergate."

"How did you get through there?" the judge asked. "Those watergates are always barred by heavy trellises."

"Part of that trellis is loose," Ma Joong replied. "A small boat can get through the gap."

"We'll have that mended first thing tomorrow," Judge Dee said. "But why are those brothels located on boats?"

"Tang told me, your honor," Hoong put in, "that

some years ago a magistrate was serving here who didn't want any brothels inside the city. Thus they had to move to boats, moored in the creek outside the east city wall. After that prudish magistrate had been transferred they stayed there, because the sailors found it convenient. They could go there directly from their ships, without having to pass the guards at the city gates."

Judge Dee nodded. Caressing his side whiskers, he observed, "That Po Kai sounds an interesting fellow, I'd like to meet him sometime."

"He may be a poet," Chiao Tai said, "but he's a clever customer all the same. He placed us at a glance as ex-highwaymen, and on the boat he was the only one who noticed they were beating up that girl."

"Beating up a girl?" Judge Dee asked, astonished.

Chiao Tai hit his fist on his knee. "The package!" he exclaimed. "What a fool I am! I had forgotten all about it! That Korean girl gave me a package that Magistrate Wang had entrusted to her."

The judge sat up in his chair.

"That may prove our first clue!" he said eagerly. "But why did the magistrate give it to a common prostitute?"

"Well," Chiao Tai replied, "she says Magistrate Wang met her once when she had been hired to liven up a party in a restaurant, and the old scoundrel took a liking to her. He could not of course visit her on the boat, but he often had her spend the night with him here in his own house. One day, about one month ago, when she was about to leave in the morning, he gave her a package, saying that the most unlikely place was always the best for hiding something. He told her to keep it for him, and not to tell anybody about it; he would ask for it back when he needed it. She asked what was in it, but he just laughed and said it didn't matter. Then he grew serious again, and told her that in case something should happen to him, she was to hand it over to his successor."

"Why then didn't she bring it to the tribunal after the magistrate had been murdered?" Judge Dee asked.

"Those girls," Chiao Tai replied with a shrug, "stand in deadly terror of the tribunal. She preferred to wait till someone from there would visit the boat, and I was the first who happened to come along. Here it is."

He took the flat package from his sleeve and gave it to the judge.

Judge Dee turned it around in his hands, then said excitedly, "Let's see what is inside!"

He broke the seal and quickly tore off the wrapping paper. They saw a flat box of black lacquer. The lid was decorated with a design of two bamboo stems and a cluster of leaves, beautifully molded in raised gold lacquer, and surrounded by an ornamental frame, in-laid with mother-of-pearl.

"This box is a valuable antique," Judge Dee said as he lifted the lid. Then he uttered a cry of dismay. The box was empty.

"Somebody tampered with it!" he exclaimed angrily. He quickly took up the torn paper. "I have indeed much to learn," he added peevishly. "Of course I should have examined the seal carefully before I tore off the paper! Now it's too late."

He leaned back in his chair, knitting his eyebrows.

Sergeant Hoong curiously examined the lacquer box.

"Judging by its size and shape," he said, "I would think that it was used for keeping documents in."

Judge Dee nodded.

"Well," he said with a sigh, "it's better than nothing. The dead magistrate must have put some important papers in it, more important than those he kept in the drawer of his desk. Where did the girl keep it, Chiao Tai?"

"In her cabin, in the space between her bed and

75

the wall," Chiao Tai answered promptly.

Judge Dee gave him a shrewd look.

"I see," he said dryly.

"She assured me," Chiao Tai went on quickly, to cover his embarrassment, "that she had never talked about it or shown it to anybody. But she added that when she was away the other girls used her cabin, and the servants and the guests went in and out there freely."

"That means," the judge said, "that even if your girl told the truth, practically anybody could have got at the package! Another dead end." He thought for a while, then shrugged his shoulders and went on. "Well, when I went over the books in the magistrate's library, I found a notebook. Have a look whether you can make anything of it."

He opened his drawer and gave the notebook to Ma Joong. He leafed it through, Chiao Tai looking over his shoulder. The tall fellow shook his head and gave it back to the judge.

"Couldn't we arrest some violent rogue for you, magistrate?" he asked hopefully. "My friend and me aren't too good at brain work, but we know all about the rough stuff."

"I must first identify the criminal before I can have him arrested," the judge replied with a bleak smile. "But don't worry, I have some special work for you, this very night.

"For certain reasons I must examine the back hall of the White Cloud Temple, without anybody knowing about it. Have a look again at this map, and tell me how it can be done."

Ma Joong and Chiao Tai put their heads together over the map. Pointing with his forefinger, Judge Dee said, "You see that the temple lies east of the city, on the opposite bank of the creek and south of the Korean quarter. Tang told me that the back hall of the temple is right under the wall. The hill behind it is covered by a dense forest."

"Walls can be scaled," Ma Joong remarked. "The point is, how to get behind the temple without attracting attention. There can't be many people on the road this time of the night; the guards at the east gate won't be able to keep their mouths shut when they have seen us about there so late."

Chiao Tai looked up from the map and said, "We could rent a boat behind that restaurant where we met Po Kai. Ma Joong is a good boatman, he could row us through the canal, through the gap in the watergate and then across the creek. From there on we must trust to our luck."

"That sounds like a good idea," Judge Dee said. "I'll just put on my hunting dress, then we'll go."

The four men left the tribunal by the side gate, and walked south along a main street. The weather had improved, a brilliant moon was in the sky. They found a boat moored behind the restaurant and rented it, paying a deposit.

Ma Joong proved indeed a skilled boatman. He sculled the small craft expertly to the watergate. He found the loose section in the trellis. After they had passed through, he made for the floating brothels, and brought up alongside the last boat of the row. Then he suddenly turned east, and quickly rowed across.

He selected a spot on the opposite bank where there was thick undergrowth. When the judge and Sergeant Hoong had stepped out, Ma Joong and Chiao Tai pulled the boat on land and pushed it under the shrubbery.

"We'd better leave old Hoong here, magistrate," Ma Joong said. "We can't leave the boat unattended, and there may be rough going ahead."

Judge Dee nodded and followed Ma Joong and Chiao Tai, who crept through the undergrowth. Arrived at the roadside, Ma Joong held up his hand. Parting the branches, he pointed to the thickly wooded mountain slope on the opposite side of the road. On the left they saw in the distance the marble gatehouse of the White Cloud Temple.

"I don't see anyone around," Ma Joong said. "Let's run across."

Under the trees on the other side it was pitch dark. Ma Joong took Judge Dee's hand, and helped him to get through the dense undergrowth. Chiao Tai was already ahead of them, higher up among the trees; he made hardly any noise. It was a stiff climb.

From time to time Judge Dee's guides utilized steep, narrow trails, then again pushed their way through the trees. Soon the judge had lost all sense of direction, but the two men were past masters in woodcraft and they went steadily ahead.

Suddenly Judge Dee found Chiao Tai by his side. He whispered, "We are being followed."

"I heard it too," Ma Joong said softly.

The three men stood close together, motionless. Now the judge heard also the faint, swishing sounds, and a low grunting. It seemed to come from somewhere down below on his left.

Ma Joong tugged at Judge Dee's sleeve, and lay down flat on his belly. The judge and Chiao Tai followed his example. They crept up on a low ridge. Ma Joong carefully parted the branches a little. He started to curse under his breath.

Judge Dee looked down into the shallow ravine below them. In the moonlight he saw a dark shape loping through the high sword grass.

"That must be the tiger!" Ma Joong whispered excitedly. "Pity we haven't got a crossbow. Don't worry, he won't attack three people."

"Shut up," Chiao Tai said through his teeth. He peered intently at the dark shape that moved swiftly through the grass. It jumped on a rock, then slid away under the trees.

"That isn't an ordinary beast!" Chiao Tai hissed. When he jumped, I caught a glimpse of a white, claw-like hand. It's a weretiger!"

A long, uncanny howl tore the silence. Its nearly human sound sent a cold shiver down Judge Dee's spine.

"He has smelled us," Chiao Tai said hoarsely. "Let's run for the temple; it must be right down this slope!"

He sprang to his feet, grabbing Judge Dee's arm. The two men made their way down the slope as quickly as they could, dragging the judge with them. His brain was numbed, that awful howl still resounded in his ears. He fell over a root, was pulled up again and stumbled further, the branches tearing his robes. A wild panic took hold of him; any moment he expected to feel a crushing weight falling on his back and sharp claws tearing at his throat.

Suddenly the two men let go of him and hurried ahead. When the judge had scrambled through the undergrowth, he saw a brick wall about ten feet high in front of him. Chiao Tai was already crouching against it. Ma Joong leapt lightly on his shoulders, reached for the top of the wall and pulled himself up. When he sat straddling it he bent forward and motioned to Judge Dee. Chiao Tai helped him. The judge grabbed Ma Joong's hands and he was pulled up. "Jump down!" Ma Joong snapped.

Judge Dee swung himself over the wall till he hung by his arms, then let himself go. He fell on a heap of rubbish. When he was getting up, Ma Joong and Chiao Tai jumped down by his side. In the forest beyond the wall they again heard the long drawn-out howl. Then all was silent.

They were in a small garden. Facing them was a

high hall, built on a broad brick terrace, raised about four feet above the ground.

"Well, magistrate, there's your back hall!" Ma Joong said gruffly. His heavy face was haggard in the moonlight. Chiao Tai silently inspected some tears in his robe.

Judge Dee was panting heavily; sweat poured down his face and body. With an effort he controlled his voice and said, "We'll get up on that terrace, and walk round to the entrance of the hall."

Arrived on the front side, they saw the temple complex across a large, square courtyard, paved with marble slabs. Everything was quiet as the grave.

The judge stood surveying the peaceful scene for a while, then turned and tried the heavy double door of the hall. It swung open and they saw a spacious room, dimly lit by the moonlight filtering inside through the high paper windows. It was empty but for a row of dark, oblong boxes. A faint, sickening odor of decay hung in the close air.

Chiao Tai cursed.

"Those are coffins!" he muttered.

"That's what I came for," Judge Dee said curtly. He took a candle from his sleeve and told Ma Joong to hand him his tinderbox. When he had lighted the candle, the judge crept among the coffins, reading the inscriptions on the paper labels pasted on their front sides. He halted by the side of the fourth. He rose and felt along the lid.

"It's nailed on only loosely," he whispered. "Take it down."

He waited impatiently while the two men inserted their daggers under the lid and wrenched it loose. They lifted it up and let it down on the floor. A nauseating smell rose up from the dark inside. Ma Joong and Chiao Tai shrank back with oaths.

Judge Dee hurriedly covered his mouth and nose with his neckcloth. He lifted the candle, and peered down on the face of the corpse. Ma Joong and Chiao Tai looked over his shoulder, curiosity overcoming their awe. The judge saw that this was indeed the man he had seen in the corridor: the face had the same rather haughty expression, the eyebrows were thin and straight, the nose fine, and on the left cheek there was the large birthmark. The only difference was that ugly blue spots disfigured the hollow cheeks and that the sunken eyes were closed. The judge felt a sickening hollow feeling in the pit of his stomach. The resemblance was perfect; it had been no hoax. He had met a ghost in the empty house.

He stepped back and motioned to Ma Joong and Chiao Tai to replace the lid. Then he blew out the candle.

"We had better not go back the way we came," he said dryly. "Let's follow the outer wall, and climb over it on the front side of the temple, near the gatehouse. We risk being seen, but the risk in the wood is worse!"

The two men grunted their assent.

They circled the temple compound, walking in the shadow of the wall, till they saw the gatehouse ahead. They climbed over the wall and followed the road, keeping close to the trees. They saw no one. Quickly they crossed the road, and went into the wooded patch that separated them from the creek.

Sergeant Hoong was lying on the bottom of the boat, fast asleep. Judge Dee woke him up, then helped Ma Joong and Chiao Tai to push the boat into the water.

Just as he was about to step inside, Ma Joong halted. A shrill voice came to them over the dark water. A falsetto sang, "Moon, oh silvery moon—"

A small boat was being sculled toward the watergate. The singer sat in the stern, slowly waving his arms up and down to the rhythm of his song.

"That's our drunken poet, Po Kai, going home at last!" Ma Joong growled. "Better give him time to get in ahead of us."

As the piercing voice began again, he added grimly, "At first I thought it awful. But believe me, after that howl we heard in the wood, his song sounds pretty good to me!"

EIGHT.

A RICH SHIPOWNER REPORTS THE LOSS OF HIS BRIDE; THE JUDGE RECONSTRUCTS A MEETING OF TWO PERSONS

Judge Dee was up long before dawn. He had felt exhausted on his return from the temple, but he had slept very badly. Two times he had dreamt that the dead magistrate was standing in front of his couch. But when he had woken up, drenched with perspiration, the room had been empty. At last he had risen, lighted a candle and sat at his desk, looking through the district files till the glow of dawn had reddened the paper windows and the clerk had brought him his morning rice.

When the judge laid down his chopsticks Sergeant Hoong came in with a pot of hot tea. He reported that Ma Joong and Chiao Tai had gone out already to supervise the repairing of the watergate, and to investigate the bank of the canal where they had witnessed the attack in the mist. They would try to be back in time for the morning session of the tribunal. The headman of the constables had reported that Fan Choong had still not shown up. Finally, Tang's servant had come and said that his master had had an attack of fever during the night, but would come as soon as he felt somewhat better.

"I am not feeling too well myself," Judge Dee muttered. He greedily drank two cups of hot tea, then went on. "I wish I had my books here now. There exists quite an extensive literature on ghostly phenomena and on weretigers, but unfortunately I never paid special attention to it. A magistrate can't afford to neglect any branch of knowledge, Hoong! Well, what did Tang tell you yesterday about the program for the morning session?"

"There isn't much, your honor," the sergeant replied. "We must announce the verdict in a dispute between two farmers regarding the boundary of their fields. That is all." He gave the judge a dossier.

While glancing through it Judge Dee remarked, "Fortunately, that appears quite simple. Tang has done a good job locating in the land registry that old map where the original boundaries were clearly indicated. We'll close the session as soon as we have dealt with this case. There are many more pressing affairs!"

Judge Dee rose and Sergeant Hoong helped him to don his official robe of dark green brocade. As the judge was exchanging his house bonnet for the black judge's cap with the stiffened wings, three beats on the large gong resounded through the tribunal, announcing that the morning session was about to be opened.

The judge crossed the corridor in front of his office, passed through the door behind the unicorn screen, and ascended the dais. As he sat down in the large armchair behind the bench he noticed that the court hall was crowded. The people of Peng-lai were eager to see their new magistrate.

He quickly checked whether the court personnel were in their appointed places. On either side of the bench, two clerks were sitting at lower tables, making ready their ink stones and writing brushes for taking down the proceedings. Below the platform, in front of the bench, six constables stood in two rows of three, with their headman by their side. He slowly let his heavy whip swing to and fro.

Judge Dee rapped his gavel and declared the session open. After he had finished the roll call, he turned to the documents that Sergeant Hoong had spread out on the bench. He gave a sign to the headman. Two peasants were led before the bench and quickly knelt down. The judge explained to them the tribunal's decision on the boundary problem. The peasants knocked their foreheads on the floor to express their gratitude.

The judge was about to raise his gavel for closing the session, when a well-dressed man stepped forward. As he limped to the bench, supporting himself on a heavy bamboo stick, the judge noticed that he had a rather handsome, regular face, with a small black mustache and a well-trimmed, short beard. He seemed about forty years old.

He knelt down with some difficulty, then spoke in an agreeable, cultured voice.

"This person is the shipowner Koo Meng-pin. He deeply regrets that he has to trouble your honor on the very first session over which he presides in this tribunal. The fact is, however, that I am greatly worried by the prolonged absence of my wife, Mrs. Koo, *née* Tsao, and wish to request the tribunal to initiate an investigation into her whereabouts."

He knocked his head three times to the floor.

Judge Dee suppressed a sigh. He said, "Mr. Koo shall present this court with a full account of the occurrence so as to enable it to decide what action to take."

"The wedding took place ten days ago," Koo began, "but because of the sudden demise of your honor's predecessor we refrained as a matter of course from larger festivities. On the third day my bride went back home for the customary visit to her parents. Her father is Dr. Tsao Ho-hsien, he lives upcountry, outside the west gate. My wife was to leave there the day before yesterday, on the fourteenth, and was due back here in the afternoon of that same day. When she did not come, I presumed that she had decided to prolong her stay one day. But when yesterday afternoon she still had not come, I became worried and sent my business manager, Kim Sang, to Dr. Tsao's house, to make inquiries. Dr. Tsao informed him that my wife had indeed left his house on the fourteenth, after the noon meal, together with her younger brother, Tsao Min, who trotted behind her horse. He was to have accompanied her till the west city gate. The boy had come back late that afternoon. He had told his father that when they were near the highway, he had noticed a stork's nest in a tree by the roadside. He told his sister to ride ahead, he would soon catch up with her again after he had taken a few eggs from the nest. However, when he climbed the tree a rotten branch gave way, and he fell, spraining his ankle. He limped to the nearest farm, had his foot bandaged there and was sent home on the farmer's donkey. Since when they parted his sister had been seen about to enter the highway, he had assumed that she had ridden straight back to the city."

Koo paused a moment, and wiped the perspiration from his brow. Then he resumed.

"On his way back to town my manager made inquiries in the military guardhouse, located at the crossing of the country road and the highway, and also at the farms and shops along the highway toward the city. But no one had seen a woman alone passing there on horseback that time of the day.

"Therefore this person, greatly fearing that something untoward has befallen his young bride, now respectfully begs your honor to institute a search for her without delay."

Taking a folded document from his sleeve and deferentially raising it above his head with two hands, he added, "I herewith submit a full description of my wife, the clothes she was wearing and the blazed horse she was riding."

The headman took the paper and handed it to Judge Dee. He glanced it through, then asked, "Did your wife have any jewels or large sums of money on her person?"

"No, your honor," Koo replied. "My manager asked Dr. Tsao the same question, and he stated that she had only carried a basket with cakes which his wife had given her as a present for me."

Judge Dee nodded, then asked, "Could you think of any person who has a grudge against you and might have wanted to harm your wife?"

Koo Meng-pin shook his head emphatically. He said, "There may be persons who have a grudge against me, your honor—which merchant engaged in a highly competitive trade hasn't? But none of them would dare to commit such a dastardly crime!"

The judge slowly stroked his beard. He reflected that it would be an insult to discuss publicly the possibility that Mrs. Koo had eloped with somebody else. He would have to make inquiries about the woman's character and reputation. He spoke.

"This tribunal shall at once take all necessary steps. Tell your manager to repair to my office after the session, to report in detail about his inquiries, so as to avoid double work. I shall not fail to inform you as soon as I have any news."

Then the judge rapped his gavel and closed the session.

A clerk was waiting for him in his private office. He said, "Mr. Yee Pen, the shipowner, arrived and told me he wanted to see your honor privately for a few moments. I took him to the reception hall."

"Who is that fellow?" Judge Dee asked.

"Mr. Yee is a very wealthy man, your honor," the clerk replied. "He and Mr. Koo Meng-pin are the two largest shipowners in this district; their ships go all the way to Korea and Japan. Both of them own a wharf on the river front where they build and repair their ships."

"All right," Judge Dee said. "I am also expecting another visitor, but I can see Yee Pen right now." To Sergeant Hoong he added, "You'll receive Kim Sang, and make notes about what he reports on his inquiries about his master's lost wife. I'll join you here as soon as I have heard what Yee Pen has to say."

A tall, fat man stood waiting for the judge in the reception hall. He knelt as soon as he saw Judge Dee ascending the stairs.

"We are not in the court hall here, Mr. Yee," Judge Dee said affably as he sat down at the tea table. "Rise and take this chair opposite me."

The fat man mumbled some confused excuses, then sat down gingerly on the edge of the chair. He had a fleshy, moon-shaped face with a thin mustache and a ragged ring beard. The judge did not like his small, crafty eyes.

Yee Pen sipped from his tea; he seemed at a loss how to begin.

"In a few days," Judge Dee said, "I shall invite all the notables of Peng-lai for a reception here. Then I hope to have the advantage of a longer conversation with you, Mr. Yee. I regret that just now I am rather occupied. I would appreciate it if you would forsake the formalities, and state your business."

Yee quickly made a deep bow; then he spoke.

"As a shipowner, your honor, I naturally have to follow closely all that goes on on the water front. Now I feel it my duty to report to your honor that there are persistent rumors that large quantities of arms are being smuggled out through this city."

Judge Dee sat up straight.

"Arms?" he asked incredulously. "Where to?"

"Doubtless to Korea, your honor," Yee Pen answered. "I heard that the Koreans are chafing under the defeat we inflicted on them, and are planning to attack our garrisons leaguered there."

"Have you any idea," Judge Dee asked, "who are the despicable traitors engaging in that trade?"

Yee Pen shook his head. He replied, "Unfortunately I couldn't discover a single clue, your honor. I can only say that my own ships are certainly not used for that nefarious scheme! These are just rumors, but the commander of the fort must have heard them too. They say that all outgoing ships are being searched there very strictly these days."

"If you learn anything more, don't fail to let me know at once," the judge said. "By the way, have you perhaps any idea what could have happened to the wife of your colleague Koo Men-pin?"

"No, your honor," Yee answered, "not the slightest. But Dr. Tsao will be sorry now that he didn't give his daughter to my son!" As the judge lifted his eyebrows, he added quickly, "I am one of Dr. Tsao's oldest friends, your honor, we are both adherents of a more rational philosophy, and opposed to Buddhist idolatry. Though the subject was never actually mentioned, I had always taken it for granted that Dr. Tsao's daughter would marry my eldest son. Then, three months ago when Koo's wife had died, Dr. Tsao suddenly announced that his daughter would be marrying him! Imagine, your honor, the girl is barely twenty! And Koo is a fervent Buddhist; they say he is going to offer a—"

"Quite," Judge Dee interrupted him. He was not interested in this family affair. He went on. "Last night two of my assistants met your business manager, Po Kai. He seems a remarkable fellow."

"I hope for all concerned," Yee Pen said with an indulgent smile, "that Po Kai was sober! The man is drunk half of the time, and the other half he is scribbling poetry."

"Why do you keep him then?" the judge asked, astonished.

"Because," Yee Pen explained, "that drunken poet is a genius in financial matters! It is absolutely uncanny, your honor. The other day I had reserved the whole evening for going over my accounts with him. Well, I sat down with Po Kai and started to explain. But he just took the entire sheaf of documents from my hands, made a few notes while leafing them through, and gave them back. Then he took a writing brush and wrote out neatly my balance, without one mistake! The next day I told him to take a week off for drawing up an estimate for a war junk to be built for the fort. He had all the papers ready that same evening, your honor! Thus I could submit my estimate long before my friend and colleague Koo had his ready, and I got the order!" Yee Pen smiled smugly, then concluded, "As far as I am concerned, the fellow may drink and sing as much as he likes. During the little time he works for me, he earns twenty times his salary. The only things I don't like about him are his interest in Buddhism and his friendship with Kim Sang, the business manager of my friend Koo. But Po Kai maintains that Buddhism answers his spiritual needs, and that he worms much information about Koo's affairs out of Kim Sang—and that of course comes in useful, sometimes!"

"Tell him," Judge Dee said, "to come and see me one of these days. I found in the tribunal a notebook with calculations I would like to have his opinion on."

Yee Pen gave the judge a quick look. He wanted to ask something, but his host had already risen and he had to take his leave.

When Judge Dee was about to cross the courtyard he was met by Ma Joong and Chiao Tai.

"That gap in the trellis is repaired, magistrate," Ma Joong reported. "On our way back we questioned a few servants of the large mansions near the second bridge. They said that sometimes after a party they carry large baskets with garbage on a litter to the canal, and dump it into the water. But we would have to make a house-to-house investigation to find out whether some such thing happened at the time Chiao Tai and I watched the incident there."

"That'll be the explanation!" Judge Dee said, relieved. "Come with me to my office now. Kim Sang will be waiting there."

While they were walking to the office, the judge told the two men briefly about the disappearance of Mrs. Koo.

Hoong was talking to a good-looking young man about twenty-five years old. When he had presented him to the judge, the latter asked, "I presume by your name that you are of Korean descent?"

"Indeed, your honor," Kim Sang said respectfully. "I was born here in the Korean quarter. Since Mr. Koo employs many Korean sailors, he engaged me to supervise them and to act as interpreter."

Judge Dee nodded. He took Sergeant Hoong's notes of Kim Sang's story, and read them through carefully. Passing them on to Ma Joong and Chiao Tai he asked Hoong, "Wasn't Fan Choong last seen on the fourteenth, and also early in the afternoon?"

"Yes, your honor," the sergeant replied, "Fan's tenant farmer stated that Fan left the farm after the noon meal, accompanied by his manservant Woo, and went away in a westerly direction."

"You wrote here," the judge went on, "that Dr. Tsao's house is located in that same area. Let's get all this straight. Give me the district map."

When Hoong had unrolled the large pictorial map on the desk, Judge Dee took his brush and drew a circle round a section of the area west of the city. Pointing to Dr. Tsao's house, he said, "Look here now. On the

91

fourteenth, after the noon meal, Mrs. Koo leaves this house in a westerly direction. She turns right at the first crossing. Now where did her brother leave her, Kim?"

"When they were passing that small patch of wood where the two country roads join, sir," Kim Sang answered.

"Right," Judge Dee said. "Now the tenant farmer states that Fan Choong left about that same time, going in a westerly direction. Why didn't he go east, along that road that leads directly from his farm to the city?"

"On the map that looks indeed shorter, your honor," Kim Sang said, "but that road is very bad, it is just a track, and hardly usable after rain. Actually that short cut would have taken Fan longer than the detour by the highway."

"I see," Judge Dee said. Taking up his brush again, he made a mark on the stretch of road between the crossing of the country roads, and the highway.

"I don't believe in coincidences," he said. "I think we may assume that on this spot Mrs. Koo and Fan Choong met. Did they know each other, Kim?"

Kim Sang hesitated somewhat. Then he said, "Not that I know, your honor. But seeing that Fan's farm is not far from Dr. Tsao's house, I could imagine that Mrs. Koo, when she was still living with her parents, would have met Fan Choong."

"All right," Judge Dee said. "You gave us most useful information, Kim; we'll see what we can do. You may go now."

After Kim Sang had taken his leave, the judge looked significantly at his three assistants. Pursing his lips, he said, "If we remember what that innkeeper said about Fan, I think the conclusion is obvious."

"Koo's efforts didn't come up to the standard," Ma Joong remarked with a leer. But Sergeant Hoong looked doubtful. He said slowly, "If they eloped together, your honor, then why didn't the guards on the highway see them? There are always a couple of soldiers sitting around in front of such guard posts, and they have nothing to do but to drink tea and to stare at everybody who passes by. Moreover, they must have known Fan by sight, and they certainly would have noticed if he passed there together with a woman. And what about Fan's manservant?"

Chiao Tai had risen and now stood looking down at the map. He observed, "Whatever happened, it happened right in front of the deserted temple. And the innkeeper told some queer stories about that place! I notice that the particular stretch of road is invisible from the guard post, and also from Fan's farm, and from the house of Dr. Tsao. Neither can it be seen from the small farm where Mrs. Koo's brother had his foot bandaged. It would seem that Mrs. Koo, Fan Choong and his servant disappeared on that stretch of road into thin air!"

Judge Dee rose abruptly. He said, "It's no use theorizing before we have examined that area ourselves, and talked with Dr. Tsao and Fan's tenant farmer. The sky is clear for once; let's go out there now! After last night's experiences, I feel I could do with a nice ride through the country in broad daylight!"

NINE.

JUDGE DEE TAKES HIS MEN TO INSPECT
A FARMHOUSE; A STRANGE DISCOVERY
IS MADE IN THE MULBERRY BUSH

The peasants working in the fields outside the west city
gate lifted their heads and gaped at the cavalcade they
saw passing along the mud road. Judge Dee rode in
front, followed by Sergeant Hoong, Ma Joong and
Chiao Tai. Behind them came the headman of the constables with ten of his men, all on horseback.

Judge Dee had decided to take the short cut to Fan
Choong's farm. But he soon saw that Kim Sang had
been right, it was a very bad road indeed. The dried
mud had hardened into deep furrows, their horses had
to step slowly, and mostly they rode in single file.

When they had passed a patch of mulberry trees, the
headman forced his horse into the field and rode up to
the judge. Pointing at a small farmhouse standing on
an elevated spot ahead he said officiously, "That is Fan's
farm, your honor!"

Giving him a sour look, Judge Dee said sternly, "I
won't have you trample the peasants' good fields, headman! I know that is Fan's farm, because I took the
trouble to look at the map."

The crestfallen headman waited till Judge Dee's
three assistants had passed him. Then he muttered to
the eldest of his men, "What a martinet we have got!
And those two bullies he has brought along! Yesterday

they made me take part in the drill, me, the headman!"

"It's a hard life," the constable sighed. "And I, I don't have relatives who leave me a snug little farm."

When they had come to a small thatched hut by the roadside, Judge Dee jumped from his horse. From there a winding path went up to the farm. The judge ordered the headman to wait there with his men while he and

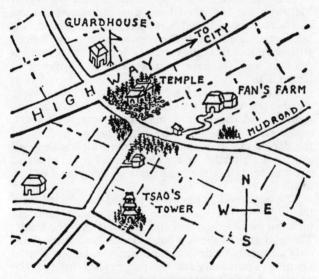

A SECTION OF THE DISTRICT PENG-LAI

his three assistants went on to the farmhouse on foot.

Passing in front of the hut, Ma Joong kicked the door open, revealing a large pile of faggots.

"You never know!" he remarked and made to pull the door shut again.

But Judge Dee pushed him aside, he had seen some-

95

thing white among the dry branches. He picked it up and showed it to the others. It was a woman's embroidered handkerchief; it still smelled faintly of musk.

"The women in the fields don't use these as a rule," the judge remarked as he put it carefully away in his sleeve.

The four men walked up to the farmhouse. About halfway a sturdy girl, clad in a blue jacket and trousers and with a colored cloth wrapped round her head, was busy weeding the field. She righted herself and looked with open mouth at the men. Ma Joong gave her an appraising look. "I have seen worse," he whispered to Chiao Tai.

The farmhouse was a low building of two rooms. Against the wall there was a kind of porch, with a large toolbox underneath it. A barn stood somewhat apart, separated from the house by a high hedge. In front of the door a tall man clad in a patched blue robe stood sharpening a scythe. Judge Dee stepped up to him and said curtly, "I am the magistrate of Peng-lai. Lead us inside."

The small eyes in the man's rugged face darted from the judge to the three men accompanying him. He made an awkward bow, then took them into the house. The plaster wall showed bare patches, and there stood only a roughly made deal table and two rickety chairs. Leaning against the table, Judge Dee ordered the peasant to state his name and those of the other people living there.

"This person," the peasant said in a surly voice, "is called Pei Chiu, tenant farmer of Master Fan Choong, of the tribunal. The wife died two years ago. I only have my daughter Soo-niang here. She cooks and helps me working the field."

"It seems quite a farm for one man," the judge remarked.

"When I have money," Pei Chiu muttered, "I hire a hand. But that isn't often. Fan is a hard taskmaster."

He gave the judge a defiant look from under his tufted eyebrows. Judge Dee thought that this swarthy fellow with his broad, bent shoulders and his long muscular arms did not look very prepossessing. He said, "Tell me about your landlord's visit."

Pei Chiu plucked at the frayed edge of his faded collar.

"He came here on the fourteenth," he replied gruffly. "Me and Soo-niang had just eaten our noon rice. I ask him for money for buying a new supply of seed. He says no. He says to Woo to go have a look in the barn. The bastard says there is still half a sack of seed. The master laughs. Then they leave, riding west to the highway. That is all. I have told that already to the constable."

He looked at the floor.

Judge Dee studied him silently. Suddenly he barked, "Look at your magistrate, Pei Chiu! Tell me, what happened to the woman?"

The peasant gave the judge a startled look. Then he swung round and darted to the door. Ma Joong sprang after him, grabbed his collar and dragged him back. He forced him down on his knees in front of the judge.

"I didn't do it!" he shouted.

"I know exactly what happened here!" Judge Dee snapped. "Don't lie to me!"

"I can explain everything, excellency," Pei Chiu wailed, wringing his hands.

"Speak up then," Judge Dee said curtly.

Pei Chiu wrinkled his low forehead. He took a deep breath, then began slowly.

"It was like this. The same day as I said, Woo comes up here leading three horses. He says the master and his wife will stay the night on the farm. I don't know the master has married, but I don't ask. Woo is a bastard. I

97

call Soo-niang. I tell her to kill a chicken, for I know the master is coming for the rent. I tell her to make the master's bedroom ready and to fry that chicken with a piece of garlic. Then I take the horses to the barn. I rub them off and I feed them.

"When I come back to the house, the master is sitting at the table here. The red cashbox is standing in front of him. I know he wants the rent. I say I haven't got it, I had bought new seed. He curses me, then he tells Woo to look if there are sacks with seed in the barn. Then, he says, I must show Woo all over our fields.

"When we come back to the house, it's getting dark. The master shouts from the bedroom that he wants food. Soo-niang takes it there. I eat a bowl of gruel with Woo, in front of the barn. Woo says I'll have to pay him fifty coppers, then he'll say that I tend the fields well. I give him the coppers, then Woo goes to sleep in the barn. I sit outside, thinking how I can get the rent. When Soo-niang is through cleaning the kitchen, I send her up to sleep in the loft. I lay me down to sleep next to Woo. Later I wake up. I think about the rent. Then I see that Woo is gone."

"Up to the loft," Ma Joong put in with a grin.

"I'll dispense with your levity!" Judge Dee barked at him. "Shut up and let this man tell his story."

The peasant had not noticed this byplay. Knitting his eyebrows, he went on.

"I go outside, and the three horses are gone too. I see a light in the master's bedroom. I think he is still awake, I must report to him. I knock on the door, but there's no answer. I walk round the house and see the window is open. The master and his wife are in bed. I think it's a waste to let the lamp burn when you sleep, oil being ten coppers a catty now. Then I see that the master and his wife are all covered with blood.

"I climb inside and look for the cashbox. The only thing I find is my sickle. It's lying on the floor, blood

98

all over it. I know the bastard Woo has killed them. He went away with the cashbox and the horses."

Chiao Tai opened his mouth to speak, but the judge peremptorily shook his head.

"I know they'll say I did it," Pei Chiu muttered. "I know they'll beat me till I say I did it. Then they'll chop my head off. Then Soo-niang has got no place to stay. I get my pushcart from the barn and put it under the window. I drag the bodies from the bed. That of the woman is still warm. I push them over the window sill into the cart. I push the cart to the mulberry bush, shove the bodies under the shrubbery and go back to the barn to sleep. I think that at dawn I'll go back there with a spade, and bury them properly. Next morning I go there. The bodies are gone."

"What did you say?" Judge Dee shouted. "Gone?"

Pei Chiu nodded emphatically.

"They were gone. I know someone has found them and he is gone to tell the constables. I run back to the house, pack the sickle in the master's clothes. I take the wife's robe, and wipe the bed mat and the floor with it. But I can't get the blood off the bed mat, so I take it off the bed and wrap up everything in it. I take the roll to the barn and hide it under the hay. I wake up Soo-niang and tell her all left before dawn for the city. This is the truth, I swear it's the truth, excellency! Don't let them beat me. Excellency, I didn't do it!"

He started knocking his head frantically on the floor.

The judge tugged at his mustache. Then he said to the peasant, "Rise and take us to that mulberry bush."

As Pei Chiu hurriedly scrambled up, Chiao Tai whispered excitedly to the judge.

"We met that fellow Woo on the road coming here, magistrate! Ask about the horses!"

Judge Dee ordered the peasant to describe the horses of his master and his wife. Pei said that Fan had ridden a gray horse, and Mrs. Fan a blazed one. The judge nodded and motioned Pei Chiu to move on.

A short walk brought them to a mulberry bush. Pei Chiu pointed at a spot in the undergrowth. "Here I shoved them under," he said.

Ma Joong stooped and examined the dry leaves. He gathered a few in his hands and showed them to the judge. "Those dark stains must be blood," he remarked.

"You two had better search this bush," Judge Dee said. "This dogshead is probably lying!"

Pei Chiu started to protest but the judge ignored him. Pensively playing with his side whiskers he said to Hoong, "I fear, Hoong, that this affair is not as simple as it seems. That man we met on the road didn't look like a murderer who coolly slits the throats of two people and then makes off with the money and the horses. He looked to me rather like a man in a blind panic."

After a while the sound of breaking twigs announced the return of Ma Joong and Chiao Tai. The former said excitedly, waving a rusty spade, "There's a small clearing in the middle! It looks as if something was buried there recently. I found this lying under a tree."

"Give that spade to Pei," Judge Dee said coldly. "The dogshead shall dig up himself what he has buried. Show me the way."

Ma Joong parted the undergrowth and they went among the trees, Chiao Tai dragging along the peasant, who seemed completely dazed.

In the middle of the clearing there was a patch of loose earth.

"Set to work!" the judge barked at Pei.

The peasant automatically spat in his hands, and started clearing the loose earth away. A mud-soiled white garment appeared. Aided by Chiao Tai, Ma Joong lifted a man's body out of the cavity and laid it on the dry leaves. It was the corpse of an elderly man with a closely shaved head, clad only in a thin under-garment.

"That's a Buddhist monk!" Sergeant Hoong ex-claimed.

"Go on," Judge Dee said harshly to the peasant.

Suddenly Pei Chiu let his spade drop. He gasped, "That's the master!"

Ma Joong and Chiao Tai took the naked body of a large man from the hole. They had to be careful, for the head had been nearly severed from the body. The breast was a mass of clotted blood. Looking with in-terest at the heavy muscles of the corpse, Ma Joong said with appreciation, "That was a hefty fellow!"

"Dig up your third victim!" the judge barked at Pei Chiu.

The peasant stuck his spade in the earth, but it struck a layer of rock. There was no other corpse. He looked perplexedly at the judge.

"What did you do with the woman, you rascal?" Judge Dee shouted at him.

"I swear I don't know!" the peasant cried out. "I brought here only the master and his wife, and left them under the shrubs, I never buried nothing here! I never saw that baldpate! I swear it's the truth!"

"What is happening here?" A cultured voice spoke behind the judge.

Turning round, Judge Dee saw a rotund man clad in a beautiful robe of gold-embroidered violet brocade. The lower half of his face was covered nearly entirely by a long mustache, flowing side whiskers and an enormous beard that spread out over his breast in three thick strands. On his head he wore the high gauze cap of a Doctor of Literature. He gave the judge a quick look, then put his hands respectfully in his wide sleeves and bowed deeply. He said, "This person is Tsao Ho-hsien, landowner by necessity but philos-opher by preference. I presume that your honor is our new magistrate?" As Judge Dee nodded he continued. "I was riding along here when a peasant told me that people from the tribunal were on the farm of my neighbor Fan Choong. Thus I took the liberty to come and see whether I could be of any assistance." He tried to peer past the judge at the bodies on the ground, but the judge quickly stood himself in front of him. He said curtly, "I am investigating a murder here. If you'll kindly wait awhile down by the road, I'll presently join you there."

As soon as Dr. Tsao had taken his leave with another deep bow, Sergeant Hoong said, "Your honor, there are no marks of violence on that monk's body. For all I can see he died a natural death!"

"We'll find that out this afternoon in the tribunal," the judge said. He asked the peasant, "Speak up, what did Mrs. Fan look like?"

"I don't know, excellency!" Pei Chiu wailed. "I didn't see her when she came to the farm, and when I found her body her face was all smeared with blood."

Judge Dee shrugged his shoulders. He said, "Ma Joong, you'll call the constables while Chiao Tai guards this rascal and the bodies. Have litters made of the branches here, and see to it that the bodies are conveyed to the tribunal. Put this man Pei Chiu in our jail. On your way back you go to the barn, and let Pei show you where he concealed that mat with the clothes of the victims. I'll now go back to the farm with Hoong to search the house and to question that girl."

The judge overtook Dr. Tsao as he was making his way carefully through the undergrowth, parting the branches with his long staff. His servant was waiting by the roadside, holding a donkey by the reins.

"I have to go to the farmhouse now, Dr. Tsao," Judge Dee said. "When I am through there, I shall avail myself of the opportunity to pay you a visit."

The doctor bowed deeply, the three strands of his

beard fanning out like banners. He climbed on his donkey, laid his staff across the saddle and trotted off, the servant running behind him.

"I never in all my life saw such a magnificent beard," the judge said a little wistfully to Sergeant Hoong.

Back at the house Judge Dee told Hoong to call the girl from the field. He himself went straight to the bedroom.

It contained one large bed, showing its bare wooden frame, two stools and a simple dressing table. In the corner near the door stood a small table with an oil lamp. As he looked down on the bare bed, his eye fell on a deep notch in the wooden frame, near the head. The splinters looked fresh; the notch seemed to have been made quite recently. Shaking his head in doubt, the judge went over to the window. He saw that the wooden latch was broken. When about to turn away he noticed a folded piece of paper lying on the floor, directly below the window. He picked it up and found it contained a cheap woman's comb made of bone, decorated with three round pieces of colored glass. He wrapped it up again in the paper and put it in his sleeve. He asked himself perplexedly whether two women could be involved in this case. The handkerchief he had found in the hut belonged to a lady; this cheap comb was evidently the property of a peasant woman. With a sigh he went to the sitting room, where Hoong and Pei's daughter stood waiting for him.

Judge Dee noticed that the girl was mortally afraid of him; she hardly dared to look up. He said kindly, "Well, Soo-niang, your father told me that the other day you made a very nice fried chicken for the master!"

The girl gave him a shy look, then smiled a little. The judge went on.

"Country food is much better than the stuff we get in the city. I suppose that the lady liked it too?"

Soo-niang's face fell. She said with a shrug, "She

was a proud one, was she. She sat on a stool in the bedroom and didn't even look round when I greeted her. Not she!"

"But she talked with you a bit when you were clearing the dishes away, didn't she?" Judge Dee asked.

"Then she was in bed already," the girl replied promptly.

Judge Dee pensively stroked his beard. Then he asked, "By the way, do you know Mrs. Koo well? I mean the daughter of Dr. Tsao, who recently was married in the city?"

"I saw her once or twice from afar in the fields, with her brother," the girl replied. "People say she is a nice girl, not like all those city women."

"Well," Judge Dee said, "you'll now show us the way to Dr. Tsao's house. The constables down at the hut shall give you a horse. Thereafter you may accompany us back to the city; your father is going there too."

TEN.

A PHILOSOPHER PROPOUNDS HIS LOFTY VIEWS; JUDGE DEE EXPLAINS A COMPLICATED MURDER

Judge Dee saw to his amazement that Dr. Tsao lived in a three-storied tower, built on a pine-clad hillock. He left Hoong and Soo-niang down in the small gatehouse, and followed Dr. Tsao upstairs.

While ascending the narrow staircase Dr. Tsao explained that in olden times the building had been a watchtower which had played an important role in local warfare. His family had owned it for generations, but they had always lived in the city. After the death of his father, who had been a tea merchant, Dr. Tsao had sold the house in the city and moved to the tower. "When we are up in my library, sir," he concluded, "you'll understand why."

Arrived in the octagonal room on the top floor, Dr. Tsao indicated the view from the broad window with a sweeping gesture and said, "I need space for thinking, sir! From my library here I contemplate heaven and earth, and therefrom derive my inspiration."

Judge Dee made an appropriate remark. He noticed that from the window on the north side one had a good view of the deserted temple, but that the stretch of road in front of it was concealed by the trees at the crossing.

When they were seated at the large desk piled with documents, Dr. Tsao asked eagerly, "What do they say

105

in the capital about my system, your honor?"

The judge didn't think he had ever heard Dr. Tsao's name mentioned, but he replied politely, "I heard that your philosophy is considered quite original."

The doctor looked pleased.

"Those who call me a pioneer in the field of independent thought are probably right!" he said with satisfaction. He poured the judge a cup of tea from the large teapot on the desk.

"Do you have any idea," Judge Dee asked, "what could have happened to your daughter?"

Dr. Tsao looked annoyed. He carefully arranged his beard over his breast, then answered with some asperity, "That girl, your honor, has been doing nothing but causing me bother! And I shouldn't be bothered; it affects seriously the serenity of mind I need for my work. I taught her myself to read and write, and what happened? She is always reading the wrong books. History she reads, I ask you, sir, history! Nothing but the sad records of former people who hadn't yet learned to think clearly. A waste of time!"

"Well," Judge Dee said cautiously, "often one can learn a lot from other people's errors."

"Pah!" Dr. Tsao said.

"May I ask," the judge said politely, "why you married her to Mr. Koo Meng-pin? I heard that you consider Buddhism as senseless idolatry—and to a certain degree I share that view. But Mr. Koo is a fervent Buddhist."

"Ha!" Dr. Tsao exclaimed, "that was all arranged behind my back, by the women of the two families. All women, sir, are fools!"

Judge Dee thought that a rather sweeping statement, but decided to let it pass. He asked, "Did your daughter know Fan Choong?"

The doctor threw up his arms.

"How could I possibly know that, your honor! Per-

106

haps she has seen him once or twice, for instance last month when that insolent yokel came here to speak to me about a boundary stone. Imagine sir, me, a philosopher, and . . . a boundary stone!"

"I suppose both have their uses," Judge Dee remarked dryly. When Dr. Tsao shot him a suspicious look, he went on quickly, "I see that the wall over there is covered with shelves, but that they are practically empty. What happened to all your books? You must have had an extensive collection."

"I had indeed," Dr. Tsao replied indifferently, "but the more I read the less I find. I read, yes, but only to let myself be diverted by men's folly. Every time I was through with an author, I sent his works to my cousin Tsao Fen, in the capital. My cousin, I regret to say, sir, sadly lacks originality. He is incapable of independent thought!"

The judge vaguely remembered now having met that Tsao Fen, at a dinner given by his friend Hou, the secretary of the Metropolitan Court. Tsao Fen was a charming old bibliophile, completely absorbed in his own studies. Judge Dee was going to stroke his beard but stayed his hand, annoyed, when he noticed that Dr. Tsao was already majestically caressing his own. Knitting his eyebrows, the doctor began.

"I shall now try to give you an outline, couched in simple language, and very brief, of course, of my philosophy. To begin with, I consider that the universe—"

Judge Dee quickly rose.

"I deeply regret," he said firmly, "that pressing affairs require my presence in the city. I hope soon to have an opportunity for continuing this conversation."

Dr. Tsao accompanied him downstairs. As the judge took leave of him he said, "During the noon session I'll hear some persons connected with your daughter's disappearance. You might be interested to attend."

"What about my work, sir?" Dr. Tsao asked reproachfully. "I really can't be bothered with attending sessions and so forth; it mars the serenity of my mind. Besides, Koo married her, didn't he? Her affairs are now his responsibilities. That is one of the cornerstones of my system, sir: let every man confine himself to what according to the heavenly command—"

"Good-by," Judge Dee said and jumped into the saddle.

He was riding down the hillock, followed by Hoong and Soo-niang, when suddenly a good-looking youngster stepped out among the pine trees, and bowed deeply. The judge halted his horse. The boy asked eagerly, "Is there any news about my sister, sir?"

As Judge Dee gravely shook his head, the boy bit his lips. Then he blurted out, "It was all my fault! Please find her, sir! She was so good at riding and hunting; we were always together in the field. She was far too sensible to be a girl, she ought to have been a boy." He swallowed, then went on. "We two liked it here up-country, but father is always talking about the city. But when he had lost his money—" He cast an anxious glance back at the house and added quickly, "But I shouldn't be bothering you, sir. Father'll be angry!"

"You aren't bothering me at all!" Judge Dee said quickly. He liked the boy's pleasant, open face. "It must be lonely for you now your sister is married."

The boy's face fell.

"Not more lonely than for her, sir. She told me she had no particular liking for that fellow Koo, but since she had to marry someone sometime anyway, and since father insisted so much, why not Mr. Koo? That's how she was, sir, a bit casual, but always so gay! But when she came back here the other day, she was not looking happy, and she wouldn't talk with me at all about her new life. What could have happened to her, sir?"

"I am doing all I can to find her," the judge said. Taking from his sleeve the handkerchief he had found in the hut on the farm, he asked, "Does this belong to your sister?"

"I really don't know, sir," the boy said with a smile. "All that women's stuff looks alike to me."

"Tell me," Judge Dee said, "did Fan Choong come here often?"

"He came only once to the house," the youngster replied, "when he had to see father about something. But sometimes I meet him in the field. I like him, he is very strong, and a good archer. The other day he showed me how to make a real crossbow! I like him much better than that other man from the tribunal, that old fellow Tang, who is often on Fan's farm. He looks at you in such a queer way!"

"Well," the judge said, "I'll inform your father as soon as there is news about your sister. Good-by."

When he came back to the tribunal Judge Dee ordered Sergeant Hoong to take the peasant girl to the guardhouse and look after her till the session would be opened.

Ma Joong and Chiao Tai were waiting for him in his private office.

"We found in the barn that mat with the bloodstained clothes, and the sickle," Ma Joong reported. "The woman's clothes tally with Koo's description. I sent a constable to the White Cloud Temple; he'll tell them to send someone down here for identifying the dead baldpate we found. The coroner is now examining the bodies. That clodhopper Pei we put in our jail."

Judge Dee nodded. "Has Tang reported for duty?" he asked.

"We sent a clerk to tell him about Fan," Chiao Tai replied. "He'll presently turn up here, I think. Did you find out much from that fat doctor, magistrate?"

The judge was pleasantly surprised. This was the first time that one of these two remarkable fellows had asked a question. They seemed to be getting interested in the work.

"Not much," he answered. "Only that Dr. Tsao is a pompous fool, and a liar to boot. It's quite possible that his daughter knew Fan Choong before her marriage and her brother thinks she had not been happy with Koo. Still the whole affair doesn't make sense to me. Perhaps the hearing of Pei and his daughter will bring to light some new facts.

"I'll now draw up a circular letter to all civil and military authorities of this province, asking for the arrest of that fellow Woo."

"They'll catch him when he tries to sell those two horses," Ma Joong remarked. "The horse dealers are very well organized; they keep in close contact with each other and with the authorities. They also have a system for branding horses with special marks. To sell a stolen horse is no easy job for one who is new to it. At least that's what I have always heard!" he added virtuously.

Judge Dee smiled. He took up his brush and quickly wrote out the circular letter. He called a clerk and ordered him to have it copied out and despatched at once.

Then the gong sounded and Ma Joong quickly helped the judge to don his official robe.

The news of the discovery of Fan's body had spread already; the court hall was packed with curious spectators.

The judge filled in a form for the warden of the jail, and Pei Chiu was led before the bench. Judge Dee made him repeat his statement, and the scribe read it out. When Pei had agreed that it was correct and had impressed his thumbmark on it, the judge spoke.

"Even if you told the truth, Pei Chiu, you are still guilty of failure to report and trying to conceal a murder. You shall be detained pending my final decision.

110

I shall now hear the coroner's report."

Pei Chiu was led away, and Dr. Shen came to kneel before the bench.

"This person," he began, "has carefully examined the body of a man identified as Fan Choong, chief clerk of this tribunal. I found he was killed by one blow of a sharp weapon that cut through his throat. I also examined the body of a monk, identified by Hui-pen, prior of the White Cloud Temple, as the monk Tzu-hai, almoner of the same institution. The body did show no wounds, bruises or other signs of violence, neither was there any indication that poison had been administered. I am inclined to ascribe his demise to sudden heart failure."

Dr. Shen rose and placed his written report of the autopsy on the bench. The judge dismissed him, then announced that he would interrogate Miss Pei Soo-niang.

Sergeant Hoong led her before the bench. She had washed her face and combed her hair; now she was not devoid of a certain common beauty.

"Didn't I tell you out there that she was pretty?" Ma Joong whispered at Chiao Tai. "Duck 'em in the river and they are as good as any city wench, I always say!"

The girl was very nervous, but by patient questioning Judge Dee made her tell again about Fan and the woman. Then he asked, "Had you ever met Mrs. Fan before?"

As the girl shook her head, he continued.

"How did you know then that the woman you served was indeed Mrs. Fan?"

"Well, they slept in the same bed, didn't they?" the girl replied.

Sounds of laughter arose from the crowd. Judge Dee rapped his gavel on the bench. "Silence!" he shouted angrily.

The girl had bent her head, greatly embarrassed.

111

Judge Dee's eye fell on the comb she had stuck in her hair. He took the one he had found in the bedroom of the farmhouse from his sleeve. It was an exact replica of the one Soo-niang was wearing.

"Look at this comb, Soo-niang," he said, holding it up. "I found it near the farm. Is it yours?"

The girl's round face lit up in a broad smile.

"So he did really get one!" she said with satisfaction. Suddenly she looked frightened, and covered her mouth with her sleeve.

"Who got it for you?" the judge asked gently.

Tears came in the girl's eyes. She cried, "Father'll beat me!"

"Look, Soo-niang," Judge Dee said, "you are in the tribunal here, you must answer my questions. Your father is in trouble; if you answer my questions truthfully, it may help him."

The girl firmly shook her head.

"This has got nothing to do with my father or with you," she said stubbornly. "I won't tell you."

"Speak up, or you'll get it!" the headman hissed at her, raising his whip. The girl screamed in terror, then burst out in heartbreaking sobs.

"Stay your hand!" the judge barked at the headman. Then he looked round unhappily at his assistants. Ma Joong gave him a questioning look, tapping on his breast. Judge Dee looked doubtful for a moment, then he nodded.

Ma Joong quickly stepped down from the dais, walked over to the girl and started to talk to her in an undertone. Soon the girl stopped sobbing; she nodded her head vigorously. Ma Joong whispered some more to her, then patted her encouragingly on her back, gave the judge a broad wink and resumed his position on the platform.

Soo-niang wiped her face off with her sleeve. Then she looked up at the judge and began.

112

"It was about one month ago, when we were working together on the field. Ah Kwang said I had good eyes, and when we went to the barn to eat our gruel, he said I had good hair. Father was away at the market, so I went with Ah Kwang up to the loft. Then—" She paused, then added defiantly, "And then we were in the loft!"

"I see," Judge Dee said. "And who is that Ah Kwang?"

"Don't you know?" the girl asked, astonished. "Everybody knows him! He is the day worker who hires himself out to the farmers if there's much work in the fields."

"Did he ask you to marry him?" the judge asked.

"Two times he did," Soo-niang replied proudly. "But I said no, never! 'I want a man with a piece of land of his own,' I told him. I also told him last week he couldn't come to see me secretly any more in the night. A girl must think of her future, and I'll be twenty this coming autumn. Ah Kwang said he didn't mind me marrying, but that he'd cut my throat if I ever took another lover. People may say he's a thief and a vagabond, but he was very fond of me, I tell you!"

"Now what about this comb?" Judge Dee asked.

"He did have a way with him," Soo-niang said with a reminiscent smile. "When I saw him last time, he told me he would like to give me something really nice, to remember him by. I told him I wanted a comb exactly like the one I was wearing. He said he would find one for me, even if he had to go all the way to the market in the city for it!"

Judge Dee nodded.

"That's all, Soo-niang," he said. "Have you got a place to stay here in town?"

"Auntie lives near the wharf," the girl said.

As she was led away by the sergeant, Judge Dee

113

asked the headman, "What do you know about that fellow Ah Kwang?"

"That's a violent ruffian, your honor," the headman replied immediately. "Half a year ago he was given fifty blows with the heavy whip in this tribunal for knocking down an old peasant and robbing him, and we suspect that it was he who killed that shopkeeper two months ago during a brawl in the gambling den near the west gate. He has no fixed home, he sleeps in the wood or in the barn of the farm where he happens to be working."

The judge leaned back in his chair. He played idly for a while with the comb. Then he sat up again and spoke.

"This court, having inspected the scene of the crime and having heard the evidence brought forward, opines that Fan Choong and a woman dressed in Mrs. Koo's clothes were murdered in the night of the fourteenth of this month by the vagabond Ah Kwang."

An astonished murmur rose from the audience. Judge Dee rapped his gavel.

"It is the contention of this court," he continued, "that Fan Choong's servant Woo discovered the murder first. He stole Fan's cash box, appropriated the two horses and fled. The tribunal shall take the necessary steps for the arrest of the criminals Ah Kwang and Woo.

"This tribunal shall continue its efforts to identify the woman who was with Fan, and to locate her body. It shall also try to trace the connection of the monk Tzu-hai with this case."

He rapped his gavel and closed the session.

Back in his private office the judge said to Ma Joong, "Better see that Pei's daughter gets safely to the house of her aunt. One lost woman is enough for this tribunal."

When Ma Joong had left, Sergeant Hoong said with a puzzled frown, "I didn't quite follow your honor's conclusions, just now during the session."

"Neither did I!" Chiao Tai added.

Judge Dee emptied his teacup. Then he said, "When I had heard Pei Chiu's story, I at once ruled out Woo as the murderer. If Woo had really planned to murder and rob his master, he would have done so on the way to or from Pien-foo, when he would have had better opportunities and less risk of being discovered. Second, Woo is a man from the city; he would have used a knife, certainly not a sickle, which is an extremely unwieldy weapon for a man unfamiliar with it. Third, only someone who had actually worked on that farm would have known where to find that sickle in the dark.

"Woo stole the cash box and the horses after he had discovered the murder. He feared he would be implicated in that crime, and fear combined with greed and opportunity constitutes a powerful motive."

"That seems sound reasoning," Chiao Tai remarked. "But why should Ah Kwang murder Fan Choong?"

"That was a murder by mistake," the judge replied. "Ah Kwang had succeeded in buying that second comb he had promised Soo-niang, and that night he was on his way to her. He probably thought that if he gave her the comb, she would grant him her favors once more. No doubt he and Soo-niang had agreed upon some signal whereby he could make his presence known to her. But while passing the house on his way to the barn, he saw a light in the bedroom. That was something unusual, so he pushed the window open and looked inside. Seeing in the semiobscurity the couple in the bed, he thought it was Soo-niang with a new lover. He is a violent rogue, so he went at once to the toolbox, took the sickle, jumped through the window and cut their throats. The comb dropped from his sleeve, I found it under the window. Whether he realized that

115

he killed the wrong people before he fled, I don't know."

"He probably found it out soon enough," Chiao Tai remarked. "I know his kind! He won't have left before having searched the room for something to steal. Then he must have had a second look at his victims, and discovered that the woman wasn't Soo-niang."

"But who was that woman then?" Sergeant Hoong asked. "And what about that monk?"

Knitting his bushy eyebrows, the judge replied, "I confess that I haven't the slightest idea. The dress, the blazed horse, the time of disappearance, everything points straight to Mrs. Koo. But from what her father and her brother said about her, I think I got a fair idea of her personality. Her having a liaison with that rascal Fan Choong before and after her marriage to Koo simply isn't in character. Further, granted that Dr. Tsao is a formidable egoist, I still think that his supreme indifference to his daughter's fate isn't natural. I can't rid myself of the idea that the murdered woman wasn't Mrs. Koo, and that Dr. Tsao knows it."

"On the other hand," the sergeant observed, "the woman took care that Pei and his daughter shouldn't see her face. That suggests that she was indeed Mrs. Koo, who wouldn't have wanted to be recognized. Since her brother told us that he was often out in the field together with his sister, one may assume that Pei and his daughter knew her by sight."

"That is true," Judge Dee said with a sigh. "And since Pei saw her only when her face was covered with blood, he couldn't have recognized her after the murder—if she was indeed Mrs. Koo! Well, as regards that monk, after I have taken my noon meal I shall go to the White Cloud Temple myself and try to find out more about him. Tell the guards to make my official palanquin ready, sergeant. You, Chiao Tai, shall go out this afternoon together with Ma Joong, and try

116

to find and arrest that fellow Ah Kwang. Yesterday you two offered to arrest a dangerous criminal for me. This is your chance! And while you are having a look around, you might as well go to that deserted temple and search it. It is not impossible that the dead woman was buried there; the man who stole her corpse can't have gone far."

"We'll get Ah Kwang for you, magistrate!" Chiao Tai said with a confident smile. He rose and took his leave.

A clerk came in carrying the tray with Judge Dee's noon rice. He was just taking up his chopsticks when Chiao Tai suddenly came back.

"Just now when I passed by the jail I happened to look into the cell where we temporarily deposited the two dead bodies. Tang was sitting by the side of Fan Choong's corpse, holding the dead man's hand in his own. Tears were streaming down his face. I think that's what the innkeeper meant when he said that Tang is different. It's a pathetic sight, magistrate; you'd better not go there."

He left the office.

ELEVEN.

THE JUDGE VISITS A BUDDHIST ABBOT; HE HAS A DINNER ON THE WATER FRONT

Judge Dee remained silent all the way to the east gate. Only when they were being carried across the creek over the Rainbow Bridge did he comment to Hoong on the beautiful view presented by the White Cloud Temple ahead. Its white marble gates and the blue tiled roofs stood out against the green mountain slope.

They were carried up the broad marble stairs, and the bearers deposited the palanquin in the spacious courtyard, surrounded by a broad open corridor. Judge Dee gave his large red visiting card to the elderly monk who came to meet him. "His holiness is just finishing his afternoon devotion," he said.

He led them through three other courts, each on a higher level against the mountain slope, and connected with each other by beautifully carved marble staircases.

At the back of the fourth court there was a flight of steep steps. On top Judge Dee saw a long, narrow terrace, hewn directly into the moss-covered rock. He heard the sounds of running water.

"Is there a spring here?" he asked.

"Indeed, your honor," the monk answered. "It sprang from the rock below here four hundred years ago, when the founding saint discovered the sacred statue

of the Lord Maitreya on this site. The statue is en-
shrined in the chapel there on the other side of the
cleft."

The judge saw now that between the terrace and
the high rock wall there was a cleft of about five foot
broad. A narrow bridge consisting of three transverse
wooden boards led over it to a large, dark cave.

Judge Dee stepped on the bridge and looked down
into the deep cleft. Some thirty feet below him a swift
stream gushed over pointed stones. A delightful cool
air came up from the cleft.

Inside the case on the other side of the bridge he saw
a golden trellis, with a red silk curtain hanging behind
it. That apparently concealed the holiest of the holy,
the chapel of the statue of Maitreya.

"The abbot's quarters are at the end of the terrace,"
the old monk said. He took them to a small building
with an elegantly curved roof, nestling in the shadow
of century-old trees. Soon he came out again, and bade
the judge enter. Sergeant Hoong sat down on the cool
stone bench outside.

A magnificent couch of carved ebony covered with
red silk cushions took up the entire back part of the
room. In its middle a small, rotund man was sitting
cross-legged, huddled in a wide robe of stiff gold brocade. He bowed his round, closely-shaven head, then
motioned the judge to sit down on a large carved armchair, in front of the couch. The abbot turned round
and placed the visiting card of the judge respectfully
on the small altar in the niche behind the couch. The
rest of the walls were covered by heavy silk hangings,
embroidered with scenes from the life of the Buddha.
The room was pervaded by the heavy smell of some
outlandish incense.

The old monk placed a small tea table of carved
rosewood by the side of Judge Dee's chair, and poured
him a cup of fragrant tea. The abbot waited till the

119

judge had taken a sip, then he said in a surprisingly strong, resonant voice, "This ignorant monk had intended to go to the tribunal tomorrow to pay his respects. It greatly distresses me that now your excellency has come to see me first. This monk does not deserve that signal honor."

He looked straight at the judge with friendly, large eyes. Although Judge Dee as a staunch Confucianist had little sympathy for the Buddhist creed, he had to admit that the small abbot was a remarkable personality, and had great dignity. He said a few polite words about the size and beauty of the temple.

The abbot raised his pudgy hand.

"It's all due to the mercy of our Lord Maitreya," he said. "Four centuries ago he deigned to manifest himself to this world in the shape of a sandalwood statue, more than five feet high, representing him sitting cross-legged, in meditation. Our founding saint discovered it in the cave, and thus this White Cloud Temple was built here, as guardian of the eastern part of our empire, and the protector of all seafarers." The abbot let the amber beads of his rosary glide through his fingers, softly saying a prayer. Then he resumed. "I had planned to invite your excellency personally to honor with his presence a ceremony which will soon be held in this humble temple."

"I shall deem it an honor," Judge Dee said with a bow. "What ceremony will that be?"

"The devout Mr. Koo Meng-pin," the abbot explained, "has asked permission to have a life-size copy made of the sacred statue, to be presented to the White Horse Temple, the central shrine of the Buddhist creed, in our imperial capital. He grudged no expense for having this pious work executed. He employed Master Fang, the best Buddhist sculptor in this province of Shantung, to make drawings of the sacred statue here in our temple, and to take the most careful measurements. Then Master Fang worked for three weeks in Mr. Koo's mansion sculpting the copy in cedarwood on the basis of his notes and sketches. All that time Mr. Koo treated Master Fang as his honored guest, and when the work was completed he gave a splendid feast, where Master Fang occupied the place of honor. This morning Mr. Koo had the cedarwood statue conveyed to this temple, in a beautiful case of rosewood."

The abbot nodded his round head with a satisfied smile; evidently these things meant a great deal to him. Then he resumed.

"As soon as a lucky day has been determined for the auspicious event, the copy of the statue will be solemnly consecrated in this temple. The commander of the fort has obtained permission for us that the statue shall be escorted to the capital by a detachment of lance-knights. I shall not fail to inform your excellency in advance as soon as date and hour for the consecration ceremony have been fixed."

"The calculations have just been completed, your holiness," a deep voice spoke up behind the judge. "The time will be tomorrow evening, and the hour the end of the second night watch."

A tall, spare monk stepped forward. The abbot introduced him as Hui-pen, the prior of the temple.

"Wasn't it you who identified the dead monk this morning?" Judge Dee asked.

The prior gravely inclined his head.

"It is a complete mystery to all of us," he said, "for what reason our almoner Tzu-hai visited that distant place at such an unusual hour. The only explanation would seem to be that he had been called by one of the farmers in that neighborhood on an errand of mercy and was waylaid by robbers. But I suppose that your honor has found some clues?"

121

Slowly tugging at his side whiskers, Judge Dee replied, "We think that a third person, as yet unknown, wanted to prevent at all costs the dead woman from being identified. When he happened to see your almoner passing there, he wanted to rob him of his cowl to wrap the woman's body in. You know that when he was found the almoner was clad only in his undergarment. I presume there was a scuffle, and Tzu-hai died from a sudden heart attack."

Hui-pen nodded. Then he asked, "Didn't your honor find his staff near his body?"

Judge Dee thought for a moment.

"No!" he said rather curtly. He had suddenly remembered a curious fact. When Dr. Tsao had surprised him in the mulberry bush, the doctor's hands had been empty. But when the judge overtook him on his way back to the road, he had been carrying a long staff.

"I will avail myself of this opportunity," Hui-pen continued, "to report to your honor that last night three robbers visited this temple. A monk in the gatehouse happened to see them when they climbed over the wall and fled. By the time he had raised the alarm, they had unfortunately already disappeared into the wood."

"I'll have this looked into at once," the judge said. "Could that monk give a description of them?"

"He didn't see much in the darkness," Hui-pen replied, "but he says all three were tall men, and that one had a thin, ragged beard."

"It would have helped," Judge Dee said stiffly, "if that monk had been a more observant fellow. Did they steal anything of value?"

"Being unfamiliar with the outlay of this temple," Hui-pen replied, "they searched only the back hall, and there they found only a few coffins!"

"That is fortunate," the judge remarked. To the

abbot he continued, "I shall give myself the honor of presenting myself here tomorrow night at the appointed time."

He rose and took his leave with a bow. Hui-pen and the old monk conducted him and the sergeant to the palanquin.

When they were carried back over the Rainbow Bridge, Judge Dee said to Sergeant Hoong, "I don't think we can expect Ma Joong and Chiao Tai back before nightfall. Let's make a detour along the shipyard and the wharf, outside the north gate."

Hoong gave the order to the bearers, and they were carried north along the city's second shopping street.

Outside the north gate a scene of bustling activity met their eyes. On the shipyard stood a number of hulks, supported by wooden props. Countless workmen, stripped to their loincloths, swarmed over and under the ships, and there was a loud din of shouted orders and hammer blows.

The judge had never been in a shipyard before. Walking with Hoong through the crowd, he watched everything with interest. At the end of the yard a large junk was lying turned on one side. Six workmen were lighting a grass fire under it. Koo Meng-pin and his manager, Kim Sang, were standing nearby talking to the foreman.

When Koo saw the judge and Hoong he hurriedly dismissed the foreman and came limping toward them. Judge Dee inquired curiously what the workmen were doing.

"This is one of my largest ocean junks," Koo explained. "They have careened it for burning the weeds and barnacles that have collected on its keel, and which impede its speed. Presently they'll scrape it clean, then recaulk it." As the judge stepped nearer to watch them, Koo laid his hand on his arm. "Don't go nearer, your honor!" he warned. "A few years ago a beam burst

123

loose through the heat, and fell on my right leg. The fracture never healed properly, that's why I have to support myself on this stick."

"It's a beautiful piece," the judge said with appreciation, "that speckled bamboo from the south is quite rare."

"Indeed," Koo replied, looking pleased. "It has acquired a good luster. But this kind of bamboo is really too thin for making canes, that's why I had to use two sticks, joined together." Then he went on in an undertone, "I was present at the session. Your honor's revelations have deeply disturbed me. It's terrible what my wife did, a disgrace for me and my entire family."

"You shouldn't draw hasty conclusions, Mr. Koo," Judge Dee remarked. "I was careful to stress that the identity of the woman has not yet been established."

"I deeply appreciate your honor's discretion," Koo said hurriedly. He cast a quick glance at Kim Sang and Sergeant Hoong.

"Do you recognize," the judge asked, "this handkerchief?"

Koo gave the embroidered piece of silk which Judge Dee took from his sleeve a cursory look.

"Of course," he answered. "That's one of a set I gave my wife as a present. Where did your honor find it?"

"By the roadside, near the deserted temple," Judge Dee said. "I thought—" Suddenly he fell silent. He remembered that he had forgotten to ask the abbot when and why that temple had been vacated. "Did you," he asked Koo, "hear the rumors about that temple? People say that it's haunted. That, of course, is nonsense. But if there are indeed nightly visitors, I must look into that; it is quite possible that impious monks of the White Cloud Temple are engaging in some secret mischief there. That would explain the presence of that monk near Fan's farm, perhaps he was on his way to the temple! Well, I had better go back to the White

124

Cloud Temple and ask the abbot or Hui-pen about it. By the way, the abbot told me about your pious undertaking. The consecration has been set for tomorrow night. I shall gladly attend."

Koo bowed deeply. Then he said, "Your honor can't leave here without partaking at least of a little snack! There is quite a good restaurant at the other end of the wharf, famous for its boiled crabs." To Kim Sang he said, "You can go on, you know what to do."

The judge was eager to get back to the temple, but he reflected that it might be useful to have a longer conversation with Koo. He told Hoong that he could return to the tribunal, and followed Koo.

Dusk was falling. When they entered the elegant pavilion on the waterside the waiters were already lighting the colored lampions that hung from the eaves. The two men sat down near the red-lacquered balustrade, where they could enjoy the cool breeze that came over the river and the gay sight of the colored lights in the sterns of the boats that went to and fro.

The waiter brought a large platter of steaming red crabs. Koo broke a few open for the judge. He picked out the white meat with his silver chopsticks, dipped it in a plate with ginger sauce and found it very appetizing. After he had drunk a small cup of yellow wine, he said to Koo, "When we were talking in the yard just now you seemed quite convinced that the woman on Fan's farm was your wife. I didn't like to ask you this awkward question in front of Kim Sang, but do you have any reason to suppose that she was unfaithful to you?"

Koo frowned. After a while he replied, "It's a mistake to marry a woman of quite different upbringing, your honor. I am a wealthy man, but I never had any literary education. It was my ambition to marry this time the daughter of a scholar. I was wrong. Although we were together only three days, I knew she didn't like her new life. I tried my best to understand her, but there was no response, so to speak." He suddenly added in a bitter voice, "She thought I wasn't good enough for her, and since she had been educated quite liberally, I thought that perhaps a previous attachment—"

His mouth twitched; he quickly emptied his wine cup.

"It's difficult for a third person," Judge Dee said, "to pronounce an opinion when the intimate relations between a married couple are concerned. I take it that you have good reason for your suspicions. But I for one am not convinced that the woman with Fan was your wife. I am not even sure that she was indeed killed. As to your wife, you know better than I do in what complications she may have become involved. If so, I advise you to tell me now. For her sake, and also for yours."

Koo gave him a quick glance. The judge thought he detected a glint of real fear in it. But then Koo spoke evenly.

"I have told you all I know, your honor."

Judge Dee rose.

"I see that mist is spreading over the river," he remarked. "I'd better be on my way. Thanks for this excellent meal!"

Koo conducted him to his palanquin and the bearers took him back through the city to the east gate. They walked at a brisk pace, they were eager to eat their evening rice.

The guards at the temple gate looked astonished when they saw the judge pass through again.

The first court of the temple was empty. From the main hall higher up came the sound of a monotonous chanting. Evidentally the monks were performing the evening service.

A rather surly young monk came to meet the judge.

He said that the abbot and Hui-pen were conducting the service, but that he would bring the judge to the abbot's quarters to have a cup of tea.

The two men silently crossed the empty courtyards. Arrived on the third court, Judge Dee suddenly halted in his steps.

"The back hall is on fire!" he exclaimed.

Large billows of smoke and angry tongues of fire rose high up into the air from the yard below them.

The monk smiled.

"They are preparing to cremate the almoner Tzu-hai," he said.

"I have never seen a cremation before," Judge Dee exclaimed. "Let's go there and have a look." He made for the stairs, but the young monk quickly laid his hand on his arm.

"Outsiders are not permitted to witness that ritual!" he said.

Judge Dee shook his arm free. He said coldly, "Your youth is the only excuse for your ignorance. Remember that you are addressing your magistrate. Lead the way."

In the yard in front of the back hall a tremendous fire was burning in a large open oven. There was no one about but one monk, who was busily working the bellows. An earthenware jar was standing by his side. The judge noticed also a large oblong box lying next to the oven.

"Where is the dead body?" he asked.

"In that rosewood box," the young monk said in a surly voice. "Late this afternoon the men from the tribunal brought it here on a litter. After the cremation the ashes are collected in that jar."

The heat was nearly unbearable.

"Lead me to the abbot's quarters!" the judge said curtly.

When the monk had taken him up on the terrace,

he left to look for the abbot. He seemed to have forgotten all about the tea. Judge Dee did not mind; he started pacing the terrace, the cool, moist air that came up from the cleft was a pleasant change after the fearful heat near the furnace.

Suddenly he heard a muffled cry. He stood still and listened. There was nothing but the murmur of the water below in the cleft. Then the cry was heard again, it grew louder, then ended in a groan. It came from the cave of Maitreya.

The judge went quickly up the wooden bridge leading across the entrance of the cave. When he had done two steps he suddenly froze. Through the haze rising up from the cleft he saw the dead magistrate standing at the other end of the bridge.

A cold fear gripping his heart, he stared motionless at the gray-robed apparition. The eye sockets seemed empty, their blind stare and the gruesome spots of decay on the hollow cheeks filled the judge with an unspeakable horror. The apparition slowly lifted an emaciated, transparent hand, and pointed down at the bridge. It slowly shook its head.

The judge looked down to where the ghostly hand was pointing. He only saw the broad boards of the bridge. He looked up. The apparition seemed to be dissolving into the mist. Then there was nothing.

A long shiver shook the judge. He placed his right foot carefully on the board in the middle of the bridge. The board dropped. He heard it crash down on the stones at the bottom of the cleft, thirty feet below.

He stood motionless for some time, staring at the black gap in front of his feet. Then he stepped back and wiped the cold sweat from his brow.

"I deeply regret to have kept your honor waiting," a voice said.

Judge Dee turned round. Seeing Hui-pen standing there, he silently pointed at the missing board.

"I told the abbot many times already," Hui-pen said, annoyed, "that those moldering boards must be replaced. One of these days this bridge will cause a serious accident!"

"It nearly did," Judge Dee said dryly. "Fortunately, I halted just when I was about to cross, because I heard a cry from the cave."

"Oh, they are only owls, your honor," Hui-pen said. "They have their nests near the entrance of the cave. Unfortunately, the abbot can not leave the service before he has spoken the benediction. Can I do something for your honor?"

"You can," the judge answered. "Transmit my respects to his holiness!"

He turned and walked to the stairs.

TWELVE.

THE CONFESSION OF A DISILLUSIONED LOVER; THE DISAPPEARANCE OF A KOREAN ARTISAN

When Ma Joong had brought the peasant's daughter home, her aunt, a jovial old lady, had insisted that he take a bowl of gruel there. Chiao Tai had waited for him in the guardhouse for some time, then ate his rice there together with the headman. But as soon as Ma Joong came back, they rode out together.

Outside in the street Ma Joong asked Chiao Tai, "You know what that girl Soo-niang said to me when I left there?"

"That you were a splendid fellow," Chiao Tai said indifferently.

"You don't know a thing about women, brother," Ma Joong said condescendingly. "That's of course what she was thinking, but women don't say those things, you know, at least not at the beginning. No, she said I was kind."

"Almighty heaven!" Chiao Tai shouted, aghast. "You—and kind! The poor, stupid wench! But then, I needn't worry, you don't have a chance. You haven't got a piece of land, have you? You heard her say that's what she wants."

"I have got other things," Ma Joong said smugly.

"I wish you would take your mind off the skirts, brother," Chiao Tai grunted. "The headman told me a lot about that fellow Ah Kwang. We needn't look for him inside the city; he only comes here occasionally, for drinking or gambling; he doesn't belong here. We must find him somewhere upcountry, that's where he knows his way about."

"Seeing that he's a country bumpkin," Ma Joong said, "I don't think he'll have left the district. He'll have taken to the woods west of the town."

"Why should he?" Chiao Tai asked. "As far as he knows, there's nothing to connect him with the murder. If I were in his place, I would lie low in some place nearby for a few days, and see which way the wind was blowing."

"In that case," Ma Joong said, "we might kill two birds with one stone if we begin by searching that deserted temple."

"You are right for once," Chiao Tai said wryly. "Let's go there."

They left the city by the west gate, and rode along the highway to the guardhouse at the crossing. They left their horses there, then walked to the temple, keeping to the left side of the road, where they were covered by the trees.

"The headman told me," Chiao Tai whispered when they had come to the ruined gatehouse, "that Ah Kwang is stupid in everything except woodcraft and fighting. He also has a mean way with a knife. So we had better go about this job seriously and approach that temple without his spotting us—if he is there."

Ma Joong nodded and crept into the undergrowth beside the gate, followed by Chiao Tai.

After they had struggled through the dense shrubbery for a while, Ma Joong raised his hand. Carefully parting the branches, he nodded to his friend. Together they scrutinized the high building of weatherbeaten stone that rose on the other side of a moss-overgrown court. A flight of broken stone steps led up the main entrance, just a dark opening; the doors had disappeared long ago. A couple of white butterflies fluttered about among the high-grown weeds. Apart from that nothing was stirring.

Ma Joong picked up a small stone and threw it against the wall. It clattered down the stone steps. They waited, their eyes glued on the dark entrance.

"I saw something moving inside!" Chiao Tai whispered.

"I'll slip inside there," Ma Joong said, "while you circle the temple and get in by a side gate. We'll whistle if we find something."

Chiao Tai moved away in the undergrowth on his right, Ma Joong crept in the opposite direction. When he estimated he was near the left corner of the building, he came out and stood with his back against the wall. So he moved along cautiously till he had arrived at the steps. He listened. Everything was quiet. He quickly ran up the steps, entered and stood with his back against the wall next to the door.

When his eyes had adapted themselves to the semi-obscurity he saw that the large, high hall was empty but for an old altar table against the back wall. Four thick center pillars supported the roof, connected with each other near the ceiling by heavy crossbeams.

Ma Joong left his coign of vantage and made for the door opening next to the altar. When he was passing the pillars a faint sound above his head made him look up quickly and step aside. A large dark shape came hurtling down and hit his left shoulder.

The impact threw Ma Joong on the floor with a crash that jarred every bone in his body. The large man who had tried to break his back had also fallen on the floor but he was on his feet again before Ma Joong and jumped over to him, reaching for his throat.

Ma Joong put both his feet in the man's stomach and heaved him over his head. When Ma Joong was scrambling up the other came for him again. Ma Joong aimed a kick at his groin but he side-stepped quick as lightning, went straight on and locked Ma Joong's torso in a powerful hug.

Panting heavily, each tried to get the other in a stranglehold. The fellow was as tall and strong as Ma Joong, but he was not a trained wrestler. Slowly Ma Joong forced him back toward the high altar table, making it appear as if he was unable to free his arms from the other's hold. When he had him with the small of his back against the edge of the table, Ma Joong suddenly freed his arms, passed them under those of his opponent and locked them over his throat. Raising himself on his toes, he bent the other's torso backward with the throat lock, and as the man's hands let go of him he threw his entire body weight into a powerful push. There was a sickening snapping sound, and the man's body went limp.

Ma Joong loosened his grip and let his opponent down to the floor. Panting, he stood looking down at him. The man lay quite still, his eyes closed.

Suddenly he moved his arms in a queer, futile gesture. His eyes opened. Ma Joong squatted down by his side. He knew the man was done for.

The fallen man looked at Ma Joong with small, cruel eyes. His lean, swarthy face twitched. He muttered, "I can't move my legs!"

"Don't blame me!" Ma Joong said. "Well, judging by your condition we shan't enjoy a long acquaintance, but I may as well tell you that I am an officer of the tribunal. You are Ah Kwang, aren't you?"

"You can rot in hell!" the man said. Then he started groaning.

Ma Joong went to the door, whistled on his fingers and resumed his position by Ah Kwang's side.

As Chiao Tai came running inside, Ah Kwang started to curse. Then he muttered, "That stone-throwing trick is one of the oldest in the trade."

"Your trying to jump on my neck from the roof beam isn't so new either," Ma Joong replied dryly. To Chiao Tai he added, "He won't last long."

"At least I killed that bitch Soo-niang!" the man grunted. "Sleeping with a new fellow, and that in the master's bed! For me the hay in the loft was good enough!"

"You made a slight mistake in the dark," Ma Joong said, "but I won't bother you with that now. The Black Judge in the nether world will doubtless explain everything nicely to you."

Ah Kwang closed his eyes and groaned; his breath came in gasps when he said, "I am strong. I won't die! And there was no mistake. Brother, that sickle cleft her throat till it struck the bone."

"You are a handy fellow with a sickle," Chiao Tai remarked. "Who was the fellow she was sleeping with?"

"I don't know and I don't care," Ah Kwang muttered through his clenched teeth. "But he got his too. The blood spouted from his throat, all over her too. Served the bitch right!" He began to grin but suddenly a long tremor shook his broad torso and his face went livid.

"Who was the other fellow who hung around there?" Ma Joong asked casually.

"There was nobody there but me, you stupid bastard," Ah Kwang muttered. Suddenly he looked up at Ma Joong, panic in his small eyes. "I don't want to die! I am afraid!" he said.

The two friends looked at him in respectful silence.

His face contorted in a lopsided smile. His arms twitched; then he lay still.

"The fellow is gone," Ma Joong said hoarsely. Rising, he went on. "He nearly got me, though. He was lying in wait for me, stretched out flat on one of those beams between the pillars, high up near the ceiling there. But before letting himself drop down he made a sound, and I could twist aside a bit. Just in time too. If he had landed on my neck the way he planned, he would have broken my back!"

"And now you have broken his, so that score is even," Chiao Tai said. "Let's search this temple; those are the magistrate's orders."

They went through the central and the back court-yard, and also searched the empty cells of the monks, and the wooded patch behind the temple compound. But except for some frightened field mice, they found nothing.

Back in the front hall Chiao Tai looked thought-fully at the altar table.

"Don't you remember," he asked, "that there is often a cavity behind those things where the monks hide their silver candles and incense burners in times of trouble?"

Ma Joong nodded. "We might as well have a look," he said.

They pushed the heavy table aside. In the brick wall behind it there was indeed a low, deep niche. Ma Joong stooped and looked inside. He cursed.

"The whole place is chock-full of old, broken monks' staffs," he said disgustedly.

The two friends walked out by the main gate and strolled back to the guardhouse. After they had given the corporal in charge there the necessary instructions for conveying Ah Kwang's body to the tribunal, they mounted their horses and rode back. When they passed through the west city gate, it was already dark.

They met Sergeant Hoong in front of the tribunal. He told them that he had just come back from the shipyard, where the judge was having his evening meal with Koo Meng-pin.

"I was lucky today," Ma Joong remarked. "Therefore I'll treat the two of you to a good meal in the Nine Flowers Orchard."

When they entered the restaurant they saw Po Kai and Kim Sang sitting together at a corner table. Two large wine jugs were standing in front of them. Po Kai's cap was tilted far back; he seemed in an affable mood.

"Welcome, my friends!" he shouted jovially. "Come and join us! Kim Sang has only just arrived; you can help him try to catch up with me!"

Ma Joong walked up to him and said sternly, "Last night you were drunk as an ape. You gravely insulted me and my friend, and you disturbed the peace by squealing obscene songs. I sentence you to paying for the wine! The food is on me!"

All laughed. The owner brought a simple but tasty meal, and the five men drank several rounds of wine. When Po Kai ordered a new jug, Sergeant Hoong rose and said, "We had better return to the tribunal; our judge will be back by now."

"August heaven!" Ma Joong shouted. "Of course! I must report about that temple!"

"Have you two at last seen the light?" Po Kai inquired incredulously. "Tell me, what temple has the advantage of your prayers?"

"We caught Ah Kwang in the deserted temple," Ma Joong said. "That temple is certainly deserted now; there's nothing left but a heap of broken staffs!"

"A very, very important clue!" Kim Sang said, laughing. "Your boss will like that!"

Po Kai wanted to see the three men off to the tribunal, but Kim Sang went on. "Let's stay awhile in this hospitable place, Po Kai, and drink a few more rounds."

Po Kai hesitated. Then he sat down again, saying, "All right, one tiny little last nip then. Remember that

I disapprove of insobriety."

"If there is no other work for us," Ma Joong said, "we'll drop in again later in the night, just to see how you take that last nip!"

The three men found Judge Dee sitting alone in his private office. Sergeant Hoong noticed that he was looking wan and tired. But he brightened up when he heard Ma Joong's report about the discovery of Ah Kwang.

"So my theory about the murder by mistake was right," he said. "But we still have the problem of the woman. Ah Kwang left immediately after the murder, without even taking the cashbox; he knew nothing about what happened after he had fled. That thieving servant Woo might have caught a glimpse of the third person who is certainly involved in this affair. We'll learn in due time when he has been caught."

"We made a thorough search of the entire temple and the strip of wood around it," Ma Joong said, "but we found no dead woman there. We only found behind the altar table a heap of broken staffs, like the monks are wont to carry."

The judge sat up straight in his chair.

"Monks' staffs?" he exclaimed incredulously.

"Only old, discarded ones, magistrate," Chiao Tai put in. "All of them were broken."

"What a curious find!" Judge Dee said slowly. He thought deeply. Then he roused himself and said to Ma Joong and Chiao Tai, "You two had a quite a day; you better retire now and take a good night's rest. I'll stay here and talk a bit with Hoong."

After the two stalwarts had taken their leave, Judge Dee settled back in his chair and told the sergeant about the loosened board in the White Cloud Temple. "I repeat," he concluded, "that it was a deliberate attempt at killing me."

Hoong gave his master an anxious look.

"On the other hand," he said, "that board may indeed have been wormeaten. When your honor put his weight on it—"

"I didn't!" the judge said curtly. "I just tapped it with my foot to test it." Seeing Hoong's uncomprehending look, he added quickly, "Just when I was about to step on it, I saw the ghost of the dead magistrate."

The crash of a door slamming shut somewhere in the building resounded in the room.

Judge Dee sat up abruptly.

"I told Tang to have that door mended!" he burst out angrily. With a quick look at Hoong's pale face, he took up his teacup and brought it to his lips. But he didn't drink. He stared fixedly at the small gray particles that were floating on the surface of the tea. Slowly putting the cup down again, he said tensely, "Look, Hoong, somebody has put something in my tea."

The two men looked silently at the gray powder that was slowly dissolving in the hot tea. Suddenly Judge Dee rubbed his finger over the tabletop. Then his drawn face relaxed in a wan smile.

"I am getting nervous, Hoong," he remarked wryly. "That slamming door made some plaster drop down from the ceiling. That's all."

Sergeant Hoong heaved a sigh of relief. He went to the tea table and poured out a new cup for the judge. Sitting down again, he remarked, "Perhaps after all the loose board has a natural explanation too, your honor. I can't imagine that the man who murdered the magistrate would dare to attack your honor! We haven't the slightest clue to his identity and—"

"But he doesn't know that, Hoong," the judge interrupted. "He doesn't know what suggestions the investigator may have made to me; he may think I am not proceeding against him only because I am biding my time. That unknown criminal is doubtless follow-ing all I do with close attention, and something I did or said may have given him the idea that I am on his track." The judge tugged slowly at his mustache. Then he continued. "I'll try now to expose myself as much as possible, so as to tempt him to make another try. Then he'll perhaps betray himself."

"Your honor shouldn't take that awful risk!" Hoong exclaimed, aghast. "We know he is a ruthless and in-genious scoundrel. Heaven knows what new evil scheme he is preparing now! And we don't even know—"

Judge Dee had not been listening. Suddenly he rose. Taking up the candle, he said curtly, "Come along, Hoong!"

Sergeant Hoong followed the judge as he quickly crossed the main courtyard and went to the magis-trate's private residence. He entered and silently walked through the dark corridor to the library. Stand-ing in the door, he lifted the candle and surveyed the room. It was exactly as he had left it after his former visit. Stepping up to the tea stove, he ordered Hoong, "Drag that armchair over here, sergeant!"

When Hoong had placed it in front of the tea cup-board, the judge stepped up on the seat. Lifting the candle, he scrutinized the red-lacquered roof beam.

"Give me your knife and a sheet of paper!" he said excitedly. "And hold the candle for me."

Judge Dee spread the paper out on the palm of his left hand, and with his right scraped with the tip of the knife at the surface of the beam.

Stepping down, he carefully wiped the point of the knife clean on the paper. He gave the knife back to Hoong, the paper he folded up and put in his sleeve. Then he asked Hoong, "Is Tang still in the chancery?"

"I think I saw him sitting at his desk when I came back, your honor," the sergeant replied.

The judge quickly left the library and walked over to the chancery. Two candles were burning on Tang's desk. He sat hunched in his chair, staring straight ahead of him. When he saw the two men enter he hurriedly got up.

Seeing his haggard face, Judge Dee said, not unkindly, "The murder of your assistant must have been a great shock to you, Tang. You better go back home and go to bed early. First, however, I want some information from you. Tell me, were there any repairs done in Magistrate Wang's library shortly before his death?"

Tang wrinkled his forehead. Then he replied, "No, your honor, not shortly before his death. But about two weeks earlier, Magistrate Wang told me that one of his visitors had remarked on a discolored spot on the ceiling, and promised to send along a lacquer worker to repair it. He ordered me to let that workman in when he would come to do his work."

"Who was that visitor?" Judge Dee asked tensely.

Tang shook his head.

"I really don't know, your honor. The magistrate was very popular among the notables here. Most of them used to visit him in his library after the morning session, for a cup of tea and a chat. The magistrate would make tea for them himself. The abbot, the prior Hui-pen, the shipowners Yee and Koo, Dr. Tsao and—"

"I suppose that artisan can be traced," Judge Dee interrupted impatiently. "The lacquer tree doesn't grow in these parts; there can't be many lacquer workers here in this district."

"That's why the magistrate was grateful for his friend's offer," Tang said. "We hadn't known there was a lacquer worker available here."

"Go and ask the guards," the judge ordered. "They must at least have seen that artisan! Report to me in my private office."

When he was seated again behind his desk the judge said eagerly to Sergeant Hoong, "The dust dropping in my tea supplied me with the solution. When the murderer noticed that dark spot on the ceiling, caused by the hot steam of the tea water, he realized that the magistrate always left the copper tea stove on that same spot on the cupboard, and that fact suggested to him his diabolical plan! He had an accomplice act the part of a lacquer worker. Feigning to work on the discolored spot, he drilled a small hole in the roof beam, straight above the tea stove. He put one or more small wax pills inside the hole, and those pills contained the poison powder. That was all he needed to do! He knew that the magistrate when he was engrossed in his reading would often let the tea water go on boiling some time before he rose and poured it from the pan into the teapot. Sooner or later the hot steam would melt the wax, and the pills would drop down into the boiling water. They would dissolve immediately and become invisible. Simple and effective, Hoong! Just now I found that hole in the roof beam, in the center of the discolored spot. A small quantity of wax was still sticking to its rim. So that was how the murder was committed!"

Tang came in. He said, "Two of the guards did remember the artisan, your honor. The man came to the tribunal once about ten days before the magistrate's death, when his excellency was presiding over the afternoon session. He was a Korean from one of the ships in the harbor, and could speak only a few words of Chinese. Since I had instructed the guards that they could let him in, they brought him to the library. They stayed with him there to see that he didn't pinch something. They say that the man worked for a time on the roof beam, then he climbed down his ladder and muttered something about the damage being so bad that he would have to lacquer the entire ceiling anew. He left and was never seen again."

Judge Dee leaned back in his chair.

"Another dead end!" he said disconsolately.

THIRTEEN.

MA JOONG AND CHIAO TAI GO OUT ON
A BOAT TRIP; A LOVERS' TRYST HAS
UNEXPECTED CONSEQUENCES

Ma Joong and Chiao Tai went back to the Nine
Flowers Orchard in high spirits. When they were entering the restaurant the latter said contentedly, "Now
we'll have a real good drinking bout!"

But when they walked over to the table of their
friends, Kim Sang gave them an unhappy look. He
pointed at Po Kai, who was lying with his head on the
table. A row of empty wine jugs was standing in front
of him.

"Mr. Po Kai drank too much in too great a hurry,"
Kim Sang said ruefully. "I tried to make him stop but
he wouldn't listen, and now he is in a foul temper;
there's nothing I can do with him. If you two will
kindly look after him, I'd better be off. It's a pity because that Korean girl is waiting for us."

"What Korean girl?" Chiao Tai asked.

"Yü-soo, of the second boat," Kim Sang replied.
"Today she has her night off, and she said she would
show us some interesting places in the Korean quarter,
places which even I don't know yet. I had already
hired a barge to take us out there and to have a drink
on the river. I'll go now and tell them it's all off."
He rose.

"Well," Ma Joong remarked judiciously, "we can

always try to wake him up for you and make him see reason."

"I tried," Kim Sang said, "but I warn you he is in a vile temper."

Ma Joong poked Po Kai in his ribs, then dragged him up from the table by his collar.

"Wake up, brother!" he bellowed in his ear. "Off to the wine and the wenches!"

Po Kai looked at them with bleary eyes.

"I reiterate," he spoke carefully with a thick tongue, "I reiterate that I despise you. Your company is degrading, you are nothing but a bunch of dissolute drunkards. I will have no truck with you, with none of you!"

He laid his head on the table again.

Ma Joong and Chiao Tai guffawed.

"Well," Ma Joong said to Kim Sang, "if that's the way he feels, you'd better leave him alone!" To Chiao Tai he added, "Let us have a quiet drink here. I estimate that Po Kai'll have sobered up by the time we leave."

"It seems a pity to call off the trip just because of Po Kai," Chiao Tai said. "We have never been to the Korean quarter. Why not take us along instead, Kim Sang?"

Kim pursed his lips.

"That won't be easy," he replied. "You'll have heard that there's an understanding that the Korean quarter has more or less its own jurisdiction. The personnel of the tribunal is not supposed to go there unless the warden asks for their assistance."

"Nonsense!" Chiao Tai explained. "We can go there incognito. My friend and me will take off our caps and bind up our hair, and nobody'll be the wiser."

Kim Sang seemed to hesitate, but Ma Joong shouted, "Good idea, let's go!"

As they were rising, Po Kai suddenly looked up.

Kim Sang patted him on the shoulder and said soothingly, "You'll have a nice rest here and sleep off the effects of the amber liquid."

Po Kai sprang up, overturning his chair. Pointing a wavering finger at Kim Sang, he shouted, "You promised to take me, you treacherous lecher! I may seem drunk to you, but I am not a man to be trifled with!" He resolutely picked up a wine jug by the neck and waved it threateningly at Kim Sang.

The other guests started to look at them. Ma Joong cursed roundly, quickly took the wine jug from Po Kai's hand and growled, "Can't be helped. We'll have to drag him along with us."

Ma Joong and Chiao Tai took Po Kai between them, and Kim Sang paid the bill.

Outside Po Kai began to lament tearfully, "I am very ill, I don't want to walk. I want to lie down, in a boat." He sat down in the middle of the street.

"You can't!" Ma Joong said cheerfully, dragging him to his feet again. "This morning we blocked your cozy mousehole in the watergate. You'll have to stretch your lazy legs; that'll do you good!"

Po Kai burst out crying.

"Rent a litter for him!" Chiao Tai said impatiently to Kim Sang. "Wait for us at the east gate; we'll tell the guards to let you pass!"

"I am glad you came along," Kim Sang said. "I didn't know that gap in the trellis had been repaired. I'll see you at the gate."

The two friends went east at a brisk pace. Ma Joong looked askance at his companion, who walked along silently.

"Almighty heaven!" he suddenly burst out, "don't tell me you have got it again! I must say you don't get it often, but when you get it you get it bad! How many times have I told you to stagger it, brother. A little love here, a little love there, that's the way to

145

enjoy yourself and to stay away from trouble."

"I can't help it, I like the wench," Chiao Tai muttered.

"Well, have it your own way," Ma Joong said resignedly. "But don't say later that I didn't warn you."

They found Kim Sang at the east gate, in an acrimonious argument with the guards. Po Kai was sitting up in the litter, singing a bawdy song at the top of his voice, to the undisguised delight of the chair bearers.

Chiao Tai explained to the guards that they had orders to confront Po Kai with a man on the other side of the creek. The guards looked skeptical, but they let them pass.

They paid off the litter bearers, crossed the Rainbow Bridge and hired a boat on the opposite bank. In the boat Ma Joong and Chiao Tai stuffed their black caps in their sleeves, and bound up their hair with a few pieces of tar rope.

A fairly large Korean barge was moored alongside the second boat. Garlands of colored lamps hung between the two low mats.

Kim Sang climbed on board, followed by Ma Joong and Chiao Tai, who hoisted Po Kai up.

Yü-soo was standing against the railing. She was clad in her native dress, a long straight robe of flowered white silk, bound up tightly under her breasts with a silk scarf tied in a beautiful large bow, and flaring out toward her feet. Her hair was done up in a high chignon, and she had stuck a white flower behind her ear. Chiao Tai looked at her, his eyes wide with admiration. She greeted them with a smile.

"I didn't know you two would be along too," she said. "But why do you have those queer things round your heads?"

"Hush!" Ma Joong said. "Don't tell anybody! We are disguised." Then he shouted to the fat woman on the second boat, "Hey, grandma, send my plump girl friend over! She must hold my head when I get sea-sick!"

"You'll find plenty of girls in the Korean quarter!" Kim Sang said impatiently. He barked an order in Korean to the three boatmen. They pushed the barge off, and started rowing.

Kim Sang, Po Kai and Ma Joong sat down cross-legged on the silk cushions that were lying on the deck round a low, lacquered table. Chiao Tai was going to join them but Yü-soo beckoned him to the door of the deck cabin.

"Don't you want to see what a Korean ship looks like?" she asked, pouting.

Chiao Tai gave the others a quick look. Po Kai was filling the wine cups, Kim Sang and Ma Joong were deep in conversation. He stepped over to her and said gruffly. "I don't think they'll miss me, for a while."

She looked at him with a mischievous glitter in her eyes. He thought he had never seen so beautiful a woman. She went inside and he followed her down the stairs to the main cabin.

The diffuse light of two lamps of colored silk shone on a very low, broad couch of carved ebony, lavishly decorated with inlaid mother-of-pearl, and covered with a thick, closely woven reed mat. Embroidered silk hangings decorated the walls. A thin cloud of a slightly pungent incense curled up lazily from a quaintly-shaped bronze burner on the red-lacquered dressing table.

Yü-soo went over to the dressing table and read-justed the flower behind her ear. Turning round she asked smiling, "Don't you like it here?"

Looking at her fondly, Chiao Tai felt a queer pang of sadness.

"I know now," he said hoarsely, "that one should see you always in your own surroundings and in your own native dress. But how strange that in your country women always wear white. With us white is the color of mourning."

She quickly stepped up to him and laid her finger on his lips.

"Don't say such things!" she whispered.

Chiao Tai clasped her in his arms and gave her a long kiss. Then he drew her to the couch and sat there, pulling her down by his side.

"When we are back on your boat," he whispered in her ear, "I'll stay the whole night with you!"

He wanted to kiss her again but she pushed his head away and rose. "You are not a very ardent lover, are you?" she said in a low voice.

She untied the elaborate bow below her bosom. Suddenly she moved her shoulders and the robe fell to the floor. She stood naked before him.

Chiao Tai sprang up. He took her up in his arms and laid her on the couch.

When they had been together before she had been rather passive but now she was as eager as he. He thought he had never loved a woman so much.

Their passion spent, they remained lying next to each other. Chiao Tai noticed that the barge seemed to be slowing down, they must be nearing the quay of the Korean quarter. He heard some commotion on deck. He wanted to sit up and reach for his clothes that lay in a heap on the floor in front of the couch. But Yü-soo put her soft arms round his neck from behind.

"Don't leave me yet!" she whispered.

A loud crash resounded from above, followed by angry shouts and curses. Kim Sang burst into the room, a long knife in his hand. Yü-soo's arms suddenly tightened round Chiao Tai's throat, locking his neck as if in a vice.

"Finish him off quick!" she called out to Kim Sang.

Chiao Tai gripped her arms. Trying to free his throat he succeeded in getting up in a sitting position, but the weight of the girl was dragging him down again. Kim Sang sprang to the couch, his knife poised for the thrust in Chiao Tai's breast. With a supreme effort Chiao Tai turned his torso to shake the girl off. Kim Sang struck just as the girl's body twisted across Chiao Tai's. The knife plunged into Yü-soo's exposed side. Kim Sang pulled the knife out and staggered back, staring incredulously at the blood that began to stain the girl's white skin. Chiao Tai shook his neck free of the girl's limp arms, jumped from the couch and grabbed Kim's hand with the knife. Kim came to life again. He hit a vicious blow in Chiao Tai's face that closed his right eye. But Chiao Tai now had Kim's right in both hands; he twisted it round, aiming the point of the knife at Kim's breast. Kim hit out again with his left, but at the same time Chiao Tai gave the knife a powerful thrust upward. It penetrated deeply into Kim's breast.

He threw him with his back against the wall and turned to Yü-soo. She lay half over the couch, her hand pressed on her side. A steady flow of blood was trickling through her fingers.

She raised her head and looked at Chiao with a queer, fixed stare. Her lips moved.

"I had to do it!" she faltered. "My country needs those arms; we must rise again! Forgive me—" Her mouth twitched. "Long live Korea!" she gasped. A shiver shook her body, then her head fell back.

Chiao Tai heard Ma Joong curse violently on the deck above. He rushed up, naked as he was. Ma Joong was wrestling desperately with a tall boatman. Chiao Tai locked his arms round the man's head and gave a sharp twist. As the man went limp Chiao Tai didn't loosen his hold. With a quick hip throw he heaved the body overboard.

"I took care of the other fellow," Ma Joong panted. "The third must have jumped into the water." Ma Joong's left arm was bleeding profusely.

"Come down," Chiao Tai growled. "I'll bandage that!"

Kim Sang was sitting on the floor where Chiao Tai had thrown him down, his back leaning against the wall. His handsome face was contorted; his glassy eyes were fixed on the dead girl.

Seeing Kim's lips moving, Chiao Tai bent over him and hissed, "Where are those arms?"

"Arms?" Kim Sang muttered. "That was all a hoax! Just to fool her; she believed it." He groaned, his hands twitched convulsively over the hilt of the knife protruding from his breast. Tears and sweat running down his face, he moaned, "She...she.... The swine we are!" He pressed his bloodless lips together.

"If it isn't arms, what are you smuggling?" Chiao Tai asked intently.

Kim Sang opened his mouth. A stream of blood gushed out. Coughing, he brought out, "Gold!"

Then his body sagged. He slumped sideways to the floor.

Ma Joong had been looking curiously from Kim Sang to the naked body of the dead girl. He asked, "She was going to warn you, and he killed her, hey?"

Chiao Tai nodded.

He quickly put on his robe. Then he tenderly put the girl's body straight on the couch, and covered it with her white robe. The color of mourning, he thought. Looking down on her still face he said softly to his friend, "Loyalty... That's the finest thing I know of, Ma Joong!"

"A beautiful sentiment," a voice remarked dryly behind them.

Chiao Tai and Ma Joong swung round.

Po Kai was looking from outside through the porthole, his elbows on the sill.

"Holy heaven!" Ma Joong exclaimed. "I had forgotten all about you."

"Unkind!" Po Kai commented. "I used the weapon of the weak, I fled. I let myself down on the narrow gangway that runs round this vessel."

"Come round inside here!" Ma Joong grunted. "You can help us fix my arm."

"You are bleeding like a pig," Chiao Tai said ruefully. He quickly picked up the girl's white sash and started bandaging Ma Joong's arm. "What happened?" he asked.

"Suddenly," Ma Joong replied, "one of those dogs grabbed me from behind. I wanted to duck to throw him over my head, but then the second kicked me in my stomach and drew his knife. I thought I was done for, but then the fellow who held me from behind suddenly let go. I could twist my body aside at the last moment and the knife aimed at my heart landed in my left arm. I put my knee in the fellow's groin, and placed a right under his jaw that made him crash backward through the railing. The man behind me must by that time have thought better of it and jumped overboard, I heard a splash. Then the third one was on me. It was a hefty fellow, and I couldn't use my left arm. You came just in time!"

"That'll stop the bleeding," Chiao Tai said as he knotted the ends of the sash round Ma Joong's neck. "Keep your arm in this sling."

Ma Joong winced as Chiao Tai pulled the bandage tight. Then he asked, "Where's that blasted poet?"

"Let's go up on deck," Chiao Tai said. "He's probably emptying all the wine jugs!"

But when they came up, the deck was deserted. They called Po Kai's name. The only sound that broke the stillness was the splashing of oars from afar through the mist.

With an awful curse Ma Joong ran to the stern. The dinghy was gone.

"The treacherous son of a dog!" he shouted at Chiao Tai. "He was in it too!"

Chiao Tai bit his lips. He hissed, "When we get that lying bastard I'll wring that scraggy neck of his with my own hands."

Ma Joong tried to peer through the mist that surrounded the barge.

"*If* we get him, brother," he said slowly. "I think we are somewhere down river. He has a good start, for it'll take us a long time to bring this barge back to port."

FOURTEEN.

JUDGE DEE DISCOURSES ON TWO AT-
TEMPTED MURDERS; AN UNKNOWN
WOMAN APPEARS BEFORE THE TRI-
BUNAL

It was near midnight when Ma Joong and Chiao Tai
came back to the tribunal. They had moored the
Korean barge under the Rainbow Bridge, and told the
guards of the east gate to put a few men on it to see that
nothing was disturbed.

Judge Dee was still closeted in his private office with
Sergeant Hoong. He looked up and stared amazed at
the disheveled pair.

But as Ma Joong told his story, his amazement
changed into a deep anger. When Ma Joong had finished, the judge jumped up and started pacing the
floor, his hands on his back.

"It's unbelievable!" he suddenly burst out. "Now this
murderous attack on two officers of my tribunal, directly after the attempt at eliminating me!"

Ma Joong and Chiao Tai looked astonished at
Hoong. He quickly told them in an undertone about
the loose board in the bridge over the cleft. He left out
the warning of the dead magistrate; he knew that the
occult was the only thing in the world this formidable
pair were really afraid of.

"Those dogsheads lay their traps well," Chiao Tai
observed. "Also their attack on us had been cleverly ar-

ranged. That conversation in the Nine Flowers Orchard was a carefully rehearsed scene!"

Judge Dee had not been listening. Standing still, he said, "So it's gold they are smuggling! The rumors about the arms were just a hoax to divert my attention. But what would they smuggle gold to Korea for? I had always thought there was plenty of gold there."

He angrily tugged at his beard. Sitting down behind his desk again, he resumed.

"Earlier tonight I had been discussing with Hoong why those rascals wanted me out of the way. We concluded that they must imagine that I know more about them than I actually do. But why murder you? The attack on the barge was evidently prepared after you had left Po Kai and Kim Sang. Try to remember whether during the meal you said something that might have given them cause for alarm."

Ma Joong frowned and thought deeply. Chiao Tai pensively fingered his small mustache. Then the latter said, "Well, there was the usual small talk, and quite a few jokes. But apart from that—" He shook his head disconsolately.

"I did say something about our going to that deserted temple," Ma Joong put in. "Since you had stated publicly during the session that you were going to have Ah Kwang arrested, I thought there was no harm in telling them that we got Ah Kwang there."

"Wasn't there something said also about those old staffs?" Sergeant Hoong asked.

"Yes, that's true!" Ma Joong said. "Kim Sang made a joke about it."

The judge hit his fist on the table.

"That must have been it!" he exclaimed. "For some reason or other those staffs are very important!"

He took his fan from his sleeve and started to fan himself vigorously. Then he said to Ma Joong and Chiao Tai, "Look here, couldn't you two be a bit more careful when you are tackling those rogues? Ah Kwang told us exactly what we wanted to know before he died, and those Korean boatmen probably only executed Kim Sang's orders, so with those it doesn't matter. But if you had caught Kim Sang alive, all our problems would probably have been solved!"

Chiao Tai scratched his head.

"Yes," he said ruefully, "come to think of it, it would have been nice if I had caught him alive. But it all happened rather quickly, you see. It was all over before I had realized that it had begun, so to speak!"

"Forget what I said," Judge Dee said with a smile. "I am being unreasonable. It is a pity, however, that Po Kai spied on you when you witnessed Kim Sang's death. That rascal now knows exactly what we know. If he hadn't been there, he would now be worrying himself to death whether Kim Sang betrayed the entire plot or not. And a worried criminal is liable to do foolish things and thereby give himself away."

"Couldn't we interrogate those shipowners Koo and Yee under torture?" Ma Joong asked hopefully. "After all it was their two managers who tried to murder Chiao Tai and me!"

"We haven't a shred of proof against Koo and Yee," the judge said. "The only thing we know is that Koreans play an important role in the criminal scheme, which is only to be expected since we know now that they are smuggling gold to Korea. Magistrate Wang made an unfortunate choice when he selected that Korean girl to entrust his documents to. Evidently she showed the package to her friend Kim Sang, and he removed the incriminating papers from the lacquer box. They didn't dare to destroy the box, because they feared that Magistrate Wang might have left a note among his papers stating that he gave that package to the girl; if she would be unable to produce it when

155

asked for it, she would have been arrested as a suspect. Perhaps it was for that very reason that the dead magistrate's private papers were stolen from the Court's archives. The criminals must have a very large organization indeed; they have their agents even in our imperial capital! Somehow or other they must also be concerned in the disappearance of the woman on Fan's farm, and they must have some connection with that pompous fool, Dr. Tsao. We have a number of disconnected facts, but the key that would give sense to this confused pattern of suppositions and suspicions is lacking!"

Judge Dee heaved a deep sigh. Then he said, "Well, it is past midnight; you three had better retire now and have a good rest. On your way out, sergeant, you must rouse three or four clerks from their beds, and tell them to write out placards for the arrest of Po Kai, on the charge of attempted murder, and giving his full description. Order the guards to nail those placards this very night on the gate of the tribunal, and on the big buildings all over the city, so that the people'll read them first thing in the morning. If we catch that elusive rascal, we'll probably make some headway."

The next morning when Judge Dee was taking his breakfast in his private office, attended by Sergeant Hoong, the headman came in and reported that the shipowners Koo and Yee requested an urgent interview with the magistrate.

"Tell them," the judge said curtly, "to appear at the morning session. They can say what they want to say in public."

Then Ma Joong and Chiao Tai came, followed by Tang. Tang was looking even worse than before, his face was ashen and he could hardly keep his hands still. He stammered, "This...this is awful. Never in my whole life has such an outrage occurred in this district!

An attack on two officers of the tribunal, I—"

"You needn't worry," Judge Dee said, interrupting his lamentations. "My assistants can take care of themselves."

The two friends looked pleased. Ma Joong didn't wear the sling any more, and Chiao Tai's eye looked somewhat better, though it showed all the colors of the rainbow.

While the judge was wiping his face with a hot towel, the gong sounded. Hoong helped him to change; then all proceeded to the court hall.

Despite the early hour the hall was crowded. People living near the east gate had spread the news about a fight on a Korean barge, and the citizens had read the placards for the arrest of Po Kai. While Judge Dee was calling the roll, he noticed Dr. Tsao, Yee Pen and Koo Meng-pin standing in the front row.

As soon as the judge had rapped his gavel, Dr. Tsao came forward, angrily swinging his beard. He knelt down and began excitedly.

"Your honor, last night a terrible thing happened! Late in the night my poor son Tsao Min was awakened by the neighing of our horses in the stable near the gatehouse. He went out there and found the horses very restive. He roused the gatekeeper, then took a sword and started to search among the trees round our house, thinking there might be a thief about. Then, suddenly, he felt a heavy weight falling on his back, claws dug into his shoulders. He was thrown head foremost to the ground, the last he heard was the snapping of teeth next to his neck. Then he became unconscious, because his head had struck a sharp stone. Fortunately the gatekeeper came rushing out just then with a torch; he saw a dark shape disappearing among the trees. We put our son to bed and dressed his wounds. The marks on his shoulders were not serious, but he had a gaping wound on his forehead. This morning he was conscious for a while, then he fell into delirium. Dr. Shen came at dawn, and pronounced his condition serious.

"This person must insist, your honor, that the tribunal take appropriate measures to have that man-eating tiger that roams about in our district traced and killed without delay!"

A murmur of approval rose from the audience.

"This very morning," Judge Dee said, "the tribunal shall send out hunters to look for the animal."

As soon as Dr. Tsao had withdrawn to his former place in the front row, Yee Pen came forward and knelt before the bench. After he had formally stated his name and profession, he began.

"This person read this morning the placard concerning his business manager, Po Kai. It is rumored that the said Po Kai was involved in a brawl on a Korean barge. I wish to state that the said Po Kai is a man of erratic habits and eccentric behavior, and that I must decline all responsibility for whatever he has done outside his office hours."

"When and under what circumstances did you engage the man Po Kai?" Judge Dee asked.

"He came to see me about ten days ago, your honor," Yee Pen replied, "with a letter of introduction from the famous scholar Tsao Fen, in the capital, a cousin of my good friend Dr. Tsao Ho-hsien. Po Kai stated that he had divorced his wife and wanted to stay for some time far from the capital, where his former wife's family were causing him trouble. He proved a dissolute drunkard, but of extraordinary business ability. After I had read the placard, I summoned my steward and asked him when he had last seen Po Kai. He told me that the man had come back very late last night; he had gone to his room in the fourth courtyard of my mansion, and soon after had left again, carrying a flat box. Since my steward is familiar with Po Kai's irregu-

lar habits, he took no special notice, but it did strike
him that the man seemed to be in a great hurry. Before proceeding to this tribunal I searched his room,
and found nothing missing except a leather box he
used to keep his papers in. All his clothes and personal
belongings were still there."

He paused a moment, then concluded.

"I would like to have the statement about my not
being responsible for Po Kai's unauthorized activities
placed on record, your honor!"

"It shall be recorded," Judge Dee replied coldly,
"but together with my comment, which you shall hear
now. I don't accept that statement, and herewith declare that I do hold you fully responsible for all your
manager did or did not do. He was in your service,
and lived under your roof. He took part in a carefully
prepared scheme to murder two of my assistants. It is
up to you to prove that you were not concerned in that
too!"

"How could I prove that, your honor?" Yee Pen
wailed. "I don't know anything about it, your honor!
I am a law-abiding citizen. Didn't I visit your honor the
other day especially to report that—"

"That story was a deliberate lie!" Judge Dee interrupted him harshly. "Furthermore, it has been reported
to me that queer things are going on in the vicinity of
your mansion, near the second bridge over the canal.
Until further notice you'll be under house arrest!"

Yee Pen started to protest but the headman growled
at him to keep silent. Two constables led him away to
the guardhouse, there to await Judge Dee's further
orders as to the degree to which the house arrest was
to be enforced.

When Yee Pen had been led away, Koo Meng-pin
knelt down before the bench.

"This person," he said, "takes a slightly different

159

attitude from that adopted by my friend and colleague Yee Pen. Inasmuch as his manager also, the Korean Kim Sang, was involved in the brawl on the barge, he wishes to state emphatically that he does feel that he bears the full responsibility for all activities of the said Kim Sang, including those he might engage in outside his office hours. I report to your honor that the Korean barge on which the outrage occurred was my property, and the three boatmen Korean sailors in my service. My foreman on the shipyard testified that last night, at the time of the evening meal, Kim Sang came to the wharf and ordered the barge to be rowed out, without mentioning its destination. Needless to say that he acted without my orders, and without my knowledge. But I shall personally investigate this outrage thoroughly, and I shall welcome the stationing of a few experienced men from this tribunal on the wharf and in my house, to supervise all my activities."

"This court," Judge Dee said, "appreciates Koo Meng-pin's cooperative attitude. As soon as the investigation of the brawl has been closed, the corpse of the said Kim Sang shall be transmitted to him for being conveyed to the next of kin, for burial."

The judge was about to close the session, when he noticed some commotion among the audience. A tall, coarse-faced woman in a black robe with a gaudy red pattern was pushing her way through the crowd, dragging along a veiled woman. While she knelt down, the veiled woman remained standing by her side, with bent head.

"This person," the kneeling woman said in a hoarse voice, "respectfully reports that she is Mrs. Liao, owner of the fifth flower boat, outside the east gate. She is bringing a criminal before your honor's tribunal."

The judge leaned forward and looked at the slender figure with the veil. He was rather astonished at what the woman said, for as a rule brothel owners were perfectly capable of dealing in their own way with offending prostitutes.

"What is the name of this girl," he asked, "and what is the charge you wish to bring against her?"

"She stubbornly refused to give her name, your honor!" the woman cried out, "and—"

"You ought to know," Judge Dee interrupted her sternly, "that you are not allowed to let a girl work in your establishment before you have ascertained her identity!"

The woman hurriedly knocked her forehead on the floor and wailed, "I beg your honor's pardon a thousand times! I should have begun by stating that I did not engage this girl as a prostitute. This is what happened, your honor, the complete truth! On the fifteenth, before dawn, Mr. Po Kai comes to my boat with this girl, clad in a monk's cowl. He says she is his new concubine, whom he brought home the evening before. His first wife wouldn't let her stay in the house, she ripped the girl's clothes to ribbons and insulted her and wouldn't listen to reason, although Mr. Po Kai argued with her till deep in the night. He says it'll take him a few days to talk his wife round, and that he wants to let the girl stay on my boat till he has fixed everything. He gives me some money, and tells me to get the girl a decent dress, for she has nothing on her but that cowl. Now Mr. Po Kai is a good customer, your honor, and he works for the shipowner Yee Pen, and the sailors are also such good customers, so what can a woman alone do but say yes, your honor! I give the chicken a nice dress, let her stay in a good cabin all by herself, and when my assistant says she might as well receive customers to keep in form, she won't dare to tell Mr. Po Kai anyway, I say at once no. I stand by my promises, your honor; that's the fixed policy of my house! But at the same time I always say, your honor,

161

the law comes first! So when this morning the green-grocer's boat comes alongside and the vendor tells me that placards are up for the arrest of Po Kai, I say to my assistant, 'If this wench is not a criminal herself, then she'll at least know where his excellency can find Po Kai. It's my duty to report her.' And thus I bring her here to the tribunal, your honor."

Judge Dee sat up in his chair. He spoke to the veiled woman.

"Take your veil off, state your name, and describe your relations with the criminal Po Kai."

FIFTEEN.

A YOUNG WOMAN TELLS AN AMAZING
TALE; AN OLD MAN CONFESSES A
STRANGE CRIME

The woman lifted her head and with a tired gesture raised her veil. The judge saw that she was a quite handsome girl of about twenty, with a friendly, very intelligent face. She spoke softly.

"This person is Mrs. Koo, *née* Tsao."

Astonished exclamations rose from the spectators. Koo Meng-pin quickly came forward. He gave his wife one searching look, then returned to his place in the front row, his face a deadly pallor.

"You were reported missing, Mrs. Koo," Judge Dee said gravely. "Tell exactly what happened, beginning with the afternoon of the fourteenth, when you had left your brother behind."

Mrs. Koo gave the judge a pitiful look.

"Must I tell everything, your honor?" she asked. "I would rather—"

"You must, Mrs. Koo!" the judge said curtly. "Your disappearance is connected with at least one murder, and probably with other capital offenses. I am listening."

She hesitated somewhat, then began.

"When I had taken the left turn to the highway, I met our neighbor Fan Choong, accompanied by a servant. I knew him by sight, so I saw no objection to an-

163

swering his polite greetings. He asked me where I was going, and I told him that I was on my way back to the city, and that my brother would soon be joining me. When my brother did not appear, we rode back to the crossing and looked down the road, but there was no sign of him. I assumed that since we were near the highway already, he had thought that I didn't need his escort any longer, and had walked home through the fields. Then Fan remarked that he was going to the city too, and offered to accompany me. He said he was going by the mud road; he assured me that it had been repaired and that the short cut would save us much time. Since I didn't like the idea of passing alone in front of the deserted temple, I accepted his offer.

"When we had arrived at the small hut that marks the entrance to Fan's farm, he said he had to give a message to his tenant farmer, and proposed that I rest awhile in the hut. I dismounted and sat down on the stool inside. Fan said something to his servant outside, then he came back. Looking me up and down with an evil leer, he said that he had sent his servant ahead to the farm because he wanted to spend some time alone with me."

Mrs. Koo paused a moment, an angry blush reddening her cheeks. She went on in a low voice.

"He drew me toward him but I pushed him back, warning him that I would scream for help if he didn't leave me alone. But he said laughing that I could scream my head off because nobody would hear me, and that I'd better be nice to him. He started to tear my robes off. I fought back as well as I could but he was too strong. When he had stripped me he bound my hands on my back with my sash and threw me on the heap of faggots. There I had to submit to his odious embraces. Afterward he untied my hands and told me to dress. He said he liked me, I would have to spend the night with him on his farm. He would bring me to town next day and tell my husband some good story. Nobody would ever know what had really happened.

"I knew I was at the rascal's mercy. We ate at the farm, then went to bed. As soon as Fan was fast asleep I wanted to get up and flee, and get back to my father's house. Suddenly I saw the window open, a tall ruffian climbed into the room, a sickle in his hand. In great fright I shook Fan awake, but the man sprang over to him and cut his throat with one blow of his sickle. Fan's body fell half over me, his blood spurted all over my face and breast—"

Mrs. Koo buried her face in her hands. On a sign from the judge the headman offered her a bowl of bitter tea, but she shook her head and continued.

"The man hissed, 'Now you, you treacherous slut!' Adding some horrible words, he reached over the bed, felt for my hair, drew my head back and brought the sickle down on my throat. I heard a thud by the side of my head, then I lost consciousness.

"When I came to I was lying on a cart that was bumping along an uneven road. Fan's naked corpse was lying by my side. I then realized that the point of the sickle had struck the side of the bed, so that only the edge had scratched my throat. Since the murderer evidently thought he had killed me too, I feigned to be dead. Suddenly the cart halted, it was tilted and I slid to the ground together with the corpse. The murderer threw some dry branches over us, then I heard the cart moving away. I hadn't dared open my eyes, so I can't say who the murderer was. When he entered the bedroom I thought he had a rather thin, swarthy face, but that may have been the effect of the oil lamp in the corner.

"I scrambled up and looked around. I saw in the moonlight that I was in the mulberry bush near Fan's farm. At the same time I saw a monk coming down the mud road, from the direction of the city. Since I was clad only in my loincloth I wanted to hide behind a tree, but he had already seen me and came running toward me. Leaning on his staff, he looked at Fan's corpse, then said to me, 'You killed your lover, eh? You had better come along with me to the deserted temple and keep me company a bit. Then I promise I won't betray your secret!' He wanted to grab me and I cried out in fear. Suddenly another man appeared as if from nowhere. He barked at the monk. 'Who told you you could use the temple for raping women? Speak up!' He drew a long knife from his sleeve. The monk cursed and lifted his staff. But suddenly he gasped, clutched at his heart, and fell to the ground. The other quickly bent over him. Righting himself, he muttered something about having bad luck."

"Do you think," Judge Dee interrupted, "that the newcomer knew that monk?"

"I couldn't say, your honor," Mrs. Koo replied. "It all happened so quick, and the monk didn't call him by his name. Later I learned that he is called Po Kai. He asked me what was going on. He didn't as much as glance at my nakedness, and spoke like an educated man. Since despite his shabby clothes he also had a certain air of authority about him, I decided I could trust him, and told him everything. He offered to take me home to my husband, or to my father; they would know what to do. I told him frankly that I couldn't face either of them, I was half out of my mind and wanted time to think. I asked him whether he couldn't hide me somewhere for a day or two; in the meantime he could report Fan's murder, without saying anything about me, for I was certain that the murderer had mistaken me for another woman. He replied that the murder was no concern of his, but if I wanted to hide he would help me. He added that he himself was living with other people, and that a hostel would never accept a woman alone that time of the night. The only solution he could think of was to rent a room for me in one of the floating brothels, those people asked no questions and anyway he would tell them a plausible story. He told me he would bury the bodies in the middle of the mulberry bush; it would then take several days before they would be discovered, and by that time I could decide whether I wanted to report to the tribunal on it or not. He took off the monk's cowl and told me to put it on after I had removed the blood from my face and bosom with my loincloth. When he came back I was ready. He took me to a wooded patch further along the mud road where he had tethered his horse, made me sit behind him and rode back to the city. At the canal he rented a boat, and brought me to the floating brothels outside the east wall."

"How did you pass the guards at the city gate?" the judge asked.

"He knocked on the south gate," Mrs. Koo said, "and acted as if he were very drunk. The guards knew him; he shouted something to them about importing new talent into the city. The guards told me to lift the hood, and when they saw I was indeed a woman they all laughed, made some coarse jokes about Po Kai's pranks, and let us through.

"He rented a cabin for me on the boat. I didn't hear his whispered explanation to the woman in charge there, but I saw clearly that he gave her four silver pieces. I must say she treated me well. When I told her I couldn't afford to become pregnant she even gave me a medicine to take. I gradually recovered from my fright, and decided I would wait till Po Kai would come and then ask him to take me to my father. This morning the woman came to my room together with the waiter. She said that Po Kai was a criminal and had been arrested. She added that since he had paid only a small advance for my dress and my lodging, I would have to work in the brothel to settle that debt. I told her indignantly that four silver pieces ought to cover those expenses and to spare, and that I wanted to leave there immediately. When this woman told the waiter to get her a whip, I thought that anything was better than falling into the clutches of these people, and told the woman I had witnessed the crime Po Kai had committed, and knew everything about other crimes of his. Then the woman became afraid and told the waiter that they would get into serious trouble with the authorities if they didn't report me. Thus the woman took me here to your honor's tribunal. I fully realize that I should have listened to the advice of that man Po Kai. I don't know what crime he has committed but I can only say he treated me very well. I should have reported everything at once, but I was deeply upset by what I had gone through, and the only thing I wanted was to rest and consider calmly what I should do. This is the complete truth."

While the scribe was reading out his notes of her statement, the judge reflected that she had told her story in a frank and natural manner, and that it fitted all known facts. He knew now the meaning of the deep notch he had found in the edge of the bed on the farm, and now it had also become more understandable why Ah Kwang had not realized she was not Soo-niang; for when he turned with his sickle to her, he had been standing over on Fan's side of the bed, and her face had been covered with Fan's blood. Po Kai's readiness to assist her was easily explained; it confirmed his suspicions of Dr. Tsao. Dr. Tsao must be an associate of Po Kai in his dark schemes, and the latter had doubtless informed him that his daughter had happened to witness his meeting with one of their accomplices among the monks, and that he had arranged that she would be out of their way for a few days. That also explained Dr. Tsao's indifference to his vanished daughter's fate: he knew all the time that she was safe.

After Mrs. Koo had impressed her thumbmark on the document, the judge spoke.

"You went through some fearful experiences, Mrs. Koo. I don't think anyone could honestly say that he would have acted more wisely under similar circumstances. The legalistic problem of the degree of guilt of a woman who fails to report the murder of the man who a few hours previously had committed on her the capital crime of rape, I shall not enter into. It is not my duty to provide experts in jurisprudence with material for study. It is my duty to administer justice, and to see that the damage wrought by a crime is repaired. Therefore I rule that this court has no plaint against you, and herewith restore you to your husband, Koo Meng-pin."

As Koo came forward his wife gave him a quick look. But ignoring her completely, he asked in a strained voice, "Is there any proof, your honor, that my wife was indeed raped and that she did not voluntarily submit to that scoundrel's embraces?"

Mrs. Koo gasped incredulously, but Judge Dee replied in an even voice, "There is." Taking the handkerchief from his sleeve, he added, "This handkerchief, which you yourself identified as belonging to your wife, was not found by the roadside as I previously stated, but in fact among the faggots in the hut on Fan's farm."

Koo bit his lips. Then he said, "That being so, this person does believe that his wife told the truth. But according to the code of honor observed in my humble family since generations, she should have killed herself immediately after the rape. Having failed to do so she brought shame over my house and I here state officially that I am compelled to repudiate her."

"That is your good right," Judge Dee said. "The divorce shall be duly registered. Let Dr. Tsao Ho-hsien come forward!"

169

Dr. Tsao knelt before the bench, muttering in his beard.

"Do you, Dr. Tsao," the judge asked, "agree to take your divorced daughter back to you?"

"It is my firm conviction," Dr. Tsao said in a loud voice, "that where fundamental principles are involved, one must not hesitate to sacrifice one's personal feelings. Moreover, being a man much in the public eye, I feel I must set an example to others, even if it hurts me, as a father, beyond words. Your honor, I cannot take back a daughter who has offended against our sacred moral codes."

"It shall be so recorded," Judge Dee said coldly. "Miss Tsao shall be given shelter in this tribunal, pending the completion of suitable arrangements."

He motioned Sergeant Hoong to lead Miss Tsao away. Turning to the woman of the brothel, he said, "Your attempt to force that girl to become a prostitute is a criminal offense. Since, however, you left her in peace till this morning, and since you show at least some understanding for your duties to this tribunal, I shall this time overlook that. But should any other complaint about you reach me, you'll get a whipping and your license will be suspended. That goes also for your colleagues out there. Go and tell them!"

The woman scurried away. Judge Dee rapped his gavel and closed the session.

When he left the dais it struck him that Tang was absent. He asked Ma Joong about it, who replied, "While Dr. Tsao was before the bench, Tang suddenly mumbled something about feeling ill and disappeared."

"That fellow is really becoming a nuisance!" Judge Dee said, annoyed. "If this goes on I shall have to pension him off."

Opening the door of his office, he saw Sergeant Hoong and Miss Tsao sitting there. He told Ma Joong and Chiao Tai to wait awhile outside in the corridor.

While he sat down behind his desk he said briskly to the girl, "Well, Miss Tsao, now we must see what we can do for you. What are your own wishes?"

Her lips started trembling, but soon she had mastered herself. She said slowly, "I do realize now that according to the doctrine of our sacred social order I really ought to kill myself. But I must confess that at the time the idea of suicide simply didn't occur to me." She smiled wanly, then went on. "If I was thinking of anything at all out there on the farm, it was rather of how I could go on living! It is not that I am afraid to die, your honor, but I hate to do things I can't make sense of. I beg your honor to let me have the benefit of his advice."

"According to our Confucianist doctrine," Judge Dee answered, "woman should indeed keep herself pure and undefiled. I often wonder, however, whether this pronouncement does not refer to the mind rather than to the body. Be that as it may, our Master Confucius has also said, 'Let humanity be your highest standard.' I for one am firmly convinced, Miss Tsao, that all doctrinal pronouncements must be interpreted in the light of these great words."

Miss Tsao gave him a grateful look. She thought for a while, then said, "I think the best I can do now is to enter a nunnery."

"Since you never before felt the call to enter religious life," the judge remarked, "that would only be an escape, and that isn't good enough for a sensible young woman like you. Why not let me approach a friend of mine in the capital to employ you as a teacher for his daughters? In course of time he could doubtless arrange there a suitable second marriage for you."

Miss Tsao replied shyly, "I am deeply grateful for your honor's consideration. But my brief marriage to Koo was a failure, and what happened to me on the farm, together with what I couldn't help seeing and hearing during my stay on the flower boat, all that has made me forever averse to ... the relations between men and women. Therefore I feel that a nunnery is the only right place for me."

"You are much too young to use the word 'forever,' Miss Tsao!" Judge Dee said gravely. "But it isn't meet that you and I discuss these things. In a week or two my family will be here, and I must insist that you talk over your plans thoroughly with my First Lady before you take a decision. Till then you'll stay in the house of our coroner, Dr. Shen. I hear his wife is a friendly and capable woman, and her daughter will be company for you. You'll now take Miss Tsao there, sergeant."

Miss Tsao bowed deeply, and Sergeant Hoong led her away. Then Ma Joong and Chiao Tai came in. The judge said to the latter, "You heard Dr. Tsao's complaint. I am sorry about that boy of his. I thought he was a nice youngster. Since you two are fully entitled to a day off, why don't you select a couple of hunters from among the guards and go upcountry to try to shoot that tiger? Ma Joong, you can stay here. After you have given the headman the necessary instructions for organizing with the city wardens a search for Po Kai, you can take a rest and look after your wounded arm. I won't need you two until late tonight, when all of us will have to attend that ceremony in the White Cloud Temple."

Chiao Tai agreed with enthusiasm. But Ma Joong growled at him. "You won't go without me, brother! You'll need me badly for holding the tiger by its tail while you are trying to hit it!"

The two friends laughed and took their leave.

Sitting alone at his piled desk, the judge opened the bulky dossier on the land taxes in the district. He felt he needed to distract his mind before he could settle down to a consideration of the new facts that had come to light.

He had not been reading for long, however, when there came a knock on the door. The headman entered, looking alarmed.

"Your honor," he reported excitedly, "Mr. Tang has taken poison and is dying! He wants to see you!"

Judge Dee sprang up and rushed with the headman to the gate. Crossing the street to the hostel opposite, he asked, "Is there no antidote?"

"He won't say what poison he swallowed," the headman panted. "And he waited till it was taking effect!"

In the corridor upstairs an elderly woman fell on her knees in front of the judge and implored him to forgive her husband. Judge Dee quickly said a few kind words, then she led him into a spacious bedroom.

Tang was lying in bed, his eyes closed. His wife sat down on the edge of the bed, and spoke softly to him. Tang opened his eyes; he sighed with relief as he saw the judge.

"Leave us alone," he muttered to his wife. She rose and the judge took her place. Tang gave him a long, searching look, then he spoke in a tired voice.

"This poison slowly paralyzes the body; my legs are getting numb already. But my brain is clear. I wanted to tell you about a crime I committed, and thereafter I wanted to ask you a question."

"Is there anything you didn't tell me about the magistrate's murder?" Judge Dee asked quickly.

Tang slowly shook his head.

"I told you all I know," he said. "I am too much concerned about the crimes committed by myself to worry about those of others. But that murder, and the ghostly apparition, deeply upset me. And when I am upset I can't control ... the other. Then Fan was killed, the only human being I ever really cared for, I—"

"I know about you and Fan," Judge Dee interrupted him. "We go as nature directs us. If thus two adults

173

find each other, it is their own affair. Don't worry about that."

"It isn't that at all," Tang said, shaking his head. "I only mention it to show that I was worried and nervous. And when I am feeling weak, the other inside me is too strong for me, especially when there is a bright moon in the sky." He breathed with difficulty. Heaving a deep sigh, he went on. "After all these long years I know him so well, him and all his nasty tricks! Besides, I once found a diary kept by my grandfather; he had to fight with him too. My father was free of him, but my grandfather hanged himself. He had reached the stage where he couldn't go on. Just as I have now taken poison. But now, now he'll have no place to go, for I have no children. He is going to die together with me!"

Tang's hollow face twisted in a wry smile. Judge Dee gave him a pitying look. Evidently the man's wits were wandering already.

The dying man stared ahead of him for a while. Suddenly he looked at the judge, frightened. "The poison is getting higher!" he said tensely. "I must hurry! I'll tell you how it always happens. I would wake up in the night, feeling a tightness in my chest. I would rise, start pacing the floor, up and down, up and down. But the room would become very close, I wanted fresh air. I had to go out, into the street. But the streets would narrow down, the rows of houses with their high walls would start to crowd me, try to crush me.... I would feel a fearful panic, I would gasp for breath. Then, just as I was going to suffocate, he would take over."

Tang heaved a deep sigh, he seemed to relax.

"I climbed on the city wall, and jumped down on the other side, just as I did again last night. Out in the country I felt new, vigorous blood pulsing through my veins, I felt strong and exhilarated; fresh air filled my lungs, nothing could oppose me. A new world opened for me. I smelled the different sorts of grasses, I smelled the wet earth, and I knew a hare had passed there. I opened my eyes wide, and I could see in the dark. I sniffed the air and I knew there was a pool of water among the trees ahead. Then I smelled another scent, a scent that made me crouch close to the ground, all my nerves taut. The scent of warm, red blood—"

Horrified, the judge saw the change that had come over Tang's face. His green eyes were fixing him with narrowed pupils over cheekbones that suddenly seemed broader, his mouth contorted in a snarl that bared pointed, yellow teeth; the gray mustache stood on end like a bristle. Frozen with terror, the judge saw the ears moving. Two clawlike hands came up from under the cover.

Suddenly the clawing fingers unbent, the arms fell down. Tang's face changed into a hollow death mask. He spoke in a weak voice.

"I would wake up lying in my bed again, drenched in sweat. I would rise, light a candle and hurry to the mirror. The relief, the unspeakable relief when I saw no blood on my face!" He paused, then said shrilly, "But now I tell you he is taking advantage of my weak condition, he is forcing me to take part in his vile crimes! Last night I knew I was attacking Tsao Min; I didn't want to spring on him, I didn't want to hurt him. . . . But I had to, I swear I had to, I had to—" His voice was rising to a scream.

The judge quickly laid a soothing hand on Tang's forehead, covered with cold perspiration.

Tang's scream died out in a rattle, deep in his throat. He stared at the judge in panic, frantically trying to move his lips. But only a few inarticulate sounds came out. As the judge bent over him to listen better, Tang brought out with a last effort, "Tell me . . . am I guilty?"

Suddenly a film closed over his eyes. His mouth

sagged open. His face relaxed.

The judge rose and pulled the cover over Tang's head. Now the Highest Judge would answer the dead man's question.

SIXTEEN.

JUDGE DEE GOES OUT TO EAT NOODLES IN A RESTAURANT; HE APPLAUDS THE DECISIONS OF AN ANCIENT COLLEAGUE

Judge Dee met Sergeant Hoong in front of the main entrance of the tribunal. Hoong had heard the news about Tang; he was on his way to the hostel to inquire after his condition. The judge told him that Tang had committed suicide because he had become despondent over Fan's murder. "A sinister fate persecuted Tang," he said and left it at that.

Back in his private office Judge Dee said to Hoong, "With Tang and Fan dead, we have lost the two top men of our clerical staff. Call the third scribe here, and tell him to bring along the files Tang was in charge of."

Judge Dee spent the rest of the morning with the sergeant and the scribe going through those dossiers. Tang had kept the registers of marriages, births and deaths, and of the finances of the tribunal with meticulous care, but even the brief interval of the past two days had caused arrears. Since the third scribe made a good impression, the judge appointed him provisionally in Tang's place. If he should prove satisfactory, he would be promoted, and other shifts in the clerical staff would follow.

These affairs having been attended to, Judge Dee took his noon meal outside, under the large oak tree in the corner of the courtyard. When he was drinking his tea, the headman came and reported that the search for Po Kai had thus far failed to produce any clue to his whereabouts. The man seemed to have dissolved into thin air.

Then Hoong left for the chancery to supervise the work of the clerks and to interview visitors. Judge Dee went back to his private office, let the bamboo curtains down, loosened his sash and lay down on the couch.

He felt to his dismay that the strain of the past two days had begun to tell on him. He closed his eyes and tried to relax and to order his thoughts. The disappearance of Mrs. Koo and of Fan Choong had now been solved, but he reflected that the solution of the murder of the magistrate had not progressed beyond the initial stage.

It was not that he was lacking suspects. Po Kai, Yee Pen, Dr. Tsao, and an as yet unspecified number of monks of the White Cloud Temple, including Hui-pen; the prior had appeared too soon after the abortive attempt on his life. It was clear that Yee Pen was connected with the criminal activities, but neither he nor Hui-pen nor Dr. Tsao seemed the type of person to act as their leader. The evil genius behind it all was doubtless Po Kai. He evidently was a man of many parts, and of remarkable presence of mind, and moreover a consummate actor. He had arrived in Peng-lai directly after the murder of the magistrate; it would seem that he had entrusted the preliminary work to Yee Pen and Kim Sang, then come himself from the capital to take over. But to take over what? The judge now had to admit that he must reconsider the conclusion he had arrived at together with Hoong, namely that the murderous attacks on himself and his two assistants meant that the criminals thought he knew more about their plans than he actually did. Even an imperial investigator, assisted by a number of trained secret agents, had failed to discover the truth, and the criminals certainly knew that his own investigations had brought to light only that the monks' staffs were used to smuggle gold to Korea. Evidently the gold was brought from the interior in the form of thin bars, concealed in the hollow monks' staffs. Yet the monks who traveled to Peng-lai with these loaded staffs took considerable risks, for along all the roads and highways there were at regular intervals military posts, where all nonofficial travelers were searched for contraband. Gold had to be declared, and a road tax paid for every distance covered. The profit accruing from evading the road taxes, together with the evasion of export duties in Peng-lai, couldn't possibly amount to much. The judge had the uncomfortable feeling that the gold smuggle itself was nothing but camouflage, that his opponent was enmeshing him in a clever plot, meant to divert his attention from something much more important that was going on. So important that it justified the murder of an imperial official, and the attempted murder of another. And that important thing must be scheduled to happen very soon; that was the real explanation of the criminal's brazen attacks—they were pressed for time! And he, the magistrate, didn't have the slightest idea what it was all about, while that scoundrel Po Kai had sought out and befriended Ma Joong and Chiao Tai, and thus had kept himself abreast of developments inside the tribunal. And now that elusive rascal was directing affairs from a secret hideout!

Judge Dee sighed. He wondered whether at this stage a more experienced magistrate would perhaps have taken a chance, and arrested Dr. Tsao and Yee Pen and questioned them with legal severities. But he thought he lacked sufficient proof for proceeding to such extreme measures. He could hardly arrest a man because he picked up a staff in a mulberry bush, and because he didn't show much interest in the fate of his daughter. As regards Yee Pen, he thought he had acted right. House arrest was a mild measure, sufficiently justified by his foisting on him the hoax about the arms smuggle. At the same time this deprived Po Kai of his second henchman, directly after he had lost Kim Sang. The judge hoped that this would hamper Po Kai in the execution of his plans, perhaps force him to put off his great coup, and thus give the tribunal a little more time for further investigations.

The judge reflected that events had been moving so fast that he had had no opportunity as yet for visiting the commander of the fort at the river mouth. Or should the commander come to see him first? The relations between civil and military officials were always rather delicate. If the latter were of equal rank, the civic officials as a rule took precedence over them. But the commander of the fort was probably a captain over thousand, and those were usually haughty fellows. Yet it was most important that he ascertain the commander's views on the gold smuggle. The fellow was doubtless an expert on Korean affairs; perhaps he could explain why people would want to smuggle gold to a country where it fetched, sans taxes, about the same price as in China. It was a pity he had not consulted Tang about local protocol; the poor old fellow had been a stickler for formality; he would have known. The judge dozed off.

He was awakened by loud voices in the courtyard outside. He rose quickly and straightened his robes. He noticed to his dismay that he had slept longer than he had planned, dusk was already falling.

A large group of clerks, constables and guards were standing together in the center of the courtyard. Over their heads the judge saw the tall figures of Ma Joong and Chiao Tai.

When the men respectfully made way for the magistrate, he saw four peasants lowering to the ground from their bamboo carrying poles the limp form of a very large tiger, measuring nearly ten feet in length.

"Brother Chiao got him!" Ma Joong shouted at the judge. "The peasants took us to the trail he uses in the woodland at the foot of the mountain slope. We put there a lamb as bait, and hid in the undergrowth, in a place where we were upwind. We waited and waited; it was only in the afternoon that we spotted the brute. He came for the lamb, but didn't attack it; he must have sensed danger. He lay there crouching in the grass for more than half an hour. Holy heaven what a wait that was! The lamb bleating all the time, and Brother Chiao creeping nearer and nearer, his arrow ready on his crossbow! I thought, 'If the tiger jumps now, he'll jump right on Brother Chiao's head!' I tried to creep up behind him with the two guards, our tridents ready. Suddenly the brute leapt; I saw only a streak in the air. But Brother Chiao got him, right in his flank, behind the right foreleg. Holy heaven, the arrow went in till three quarters of the shaft!"

Chiao Tai smiled happily. Pointing at the white patch that covered the huge right paw of the tiger, he remarked, "This must have been the same tiger we saw the other night on the opposite bank of the creek. I think I was a bit hasty in my conclusions, then! Though it beats me how the beast got there."

"We shouldn't worry about supernatural phenomena as long as we have our hands full with perfectly natural ones!" Judge Dee said. "Congratulations on your catch!"

"We'll now skin it," Ma Joong said. "Then we'll divide the meat among the peasants; they feed it to their children to make them strong. When we have prepared the skin, magistrate, we'll present it to you, for the armchair in your library, as a slight mark of our respect."

The judge thanked him, then he took Sergeant Hoong to the main gate. Groups of excited people were coming in, eager to see the dead tiger and the man who killed it.

"I overslept," Judge Dee said to Hoong. "It's about time for dinner. Let's go together to that restaurant where our two braves met Po Kai for the first time, and dine for a change. At the same time we might see what they say about Po Kai there. We can walk; the fresh night air may help to clear the cobwebs from my brain!"

They strolled through the busy streets in a southerly direction, and found the restaurant without difficulty. Upstairs the owner came hurriedly to meet them, his round face creased in an oily smile. He detained them long enough to give the other guests an opportunity to see what a distinguished visitor he had, then led them deferentially to a luxuriously appointed separate room, and asked what his humble kitchen might offer them. "A few quail eggs, stuffed shrimps, sliced roast pork, salted fish, smoked ham, shredded cold chicken to begin with, then—"

"Bring us," Judge Dee cut him short, "two bowls of noodles, a platter of salted vegetables and a large pot of hot tea. That's all."

"But allow me to offer your excellency at least a small cup of Rose Dew liqueur!" exclaimed the crestfallen manager. "Just to whet the appetite!"

"My appetite is excellent, thank you," said the judge. When the manager had passed on the modest order to the waiter, Judge Dee resumed. "Did Po Kai frequent this restaurant?"

"Ha!" the manager exclaimed. "I knew at once that he was a mean criminal! Always when he came in I noticed that furtive look of his, the way he put his hand in his sleeve as if he were ready to produce a dagger from it. When I heard this morning that there were placards up for his arrest, I said, 'I could have told

182

that to his excellency long ago.' "

"A pity you didn't do that then," the judge remarked dryly. He recognized in the manager that distressing type of witness, a man with no eyes and a fertile imagination. He said, "Send your headwaiter in."

The headwaiter proved to be a shrewd-looking fellow.

"I must say, sir," he began, "that I would never have thought that Mr. Po Kai was a criminal! And in my job one learns to assess the guests. He certainly seemed an educated gentleman, and that he remained, no matter how much he drank. He was always kind to the waiters, but never so as to invite familiarity. And I once overheard the head of the Classical School near the Temple of Confucius remarking on the excellent quality of his poetry."

"Did he eat or drink here often with other people?" Judge Dee asked.

"No, sir, during the ten days or so that he came here regularly he ate either alone, or with his friend Kim Sang. They were fond of making jokes together, those two gentlemen. And Mr. Po Kai's arched eyebrows gave his face such a funny expression! Sometimes, though, I noticed that his eyes weren't funny at all; they didn't belong to the eyebrows, so to speak. Then I asked myself whether he wasn't perhaps wearing some kind of disguise. But then he started laughing again, and I knew that I had been wrong."

The judge thanked him and quickly finished his noodles. He paid his bill despite the energetic protests of the manager, gave the waiters a generous tip and left.

In the street he said to Sergeant Hoong, "That waiter is an observant fellow. I greatly fear that Po Kai indeed wears a disguise. Remember that when he met Miss Tsao and didn't have to act his part, he struck her as 'having an air of authority.' He must be our main

183

opponent, the master criminal behind all this! And we can give up now all hope that our men can discover him, for he doesn't even need to hide. He just sheds his disguise, and no one recognizes him. What a pity that I never met him!"

Hoong had not heard Judge Dee's last words. He was listening intently to the sound of cymbals and flutes that came from the direction of the street where the Temple of the City God was located.

"There's a troupe of traveling actors in town, your honor!" he said excitedly. "They must have heard about the ceremony in the White Cloud Temple, and have set up their stage to make some money from the crowd that is on foot tonight. Shall we have a look, your honor?" he added hopefully.

The judge knew that the sergeant had been a devotee of the stage all his life; it was the only relaxation he ever indulged in. He nodded with a smile.

The open space in front of the temple was crowded with people. Over their heads the judge saw the high stage made of bamboo poles and matting. Red and green streamers fluttered in the air above it; actors in glittering costumes were moving about on the stage, lighted by many gaudy lampions.

The two men elbowed their way through the crowd of standing onlookers till they had reached the wooden benches of the paying audience. A heavily made-up girl in a garish stage costume took their money, and found them two empty places in the back row. Nobody paid any attention to the newcomers; all eyes were watching the stage.

Judge Dee looked casually at the four actors. He knew very little about the theatre and its conventions, but he supposed that the old man in the green brocade robe and with the flowing white beard who stood gesticulating in the center must be an elder. The two men who were standing in front of him and the woman

184

kneeling between them he could not place.

The orchestra stopped, the old man began a long recital in a high-pitched voice. The judge was unfamiliar with the queer, drawn-out theatrical diction; he could not follow it.

"What's it all about?" he asked Hoong.

The sergeant replied immediately. "The old man is the elder, your honor. The piece is nearing its end; he is now summing up a plaint the fellow on the left brought against his wife, the kneeling woman. The other man is the brother of the plaintiff; he came along to attest to his high character." He listened awhile, then continued excitedly, "The husband was away traveling for two years, and when he came back he found his wife pregnant. He brought the case before the elder, in order to obtain permission to repudiate her on the ground of adultery."

"Quiet!" a fat man sitting in front of the judge snapped over his shoulder.

Suddenly the orchestra struck up with a scraping of fiddles and clashing of cymbals. The woman rose gracefully and sang a passionate song, the contents of which escaped the judge entirely.

"She says," Sergeant Hoong whispered, "that her husband came back home late one day eight months ago, and spent the night with her. He departed again before dawn."

Pandemonium was breaking loose on the stage. All four actors sang and talked at the same time; the elder walked around in circles, shaking his head so that his white beard fluttered around him. The husband turned to face the audience; waving his arms, he sang in a strident voice that his wife was lying. The forefinger of his right hand had been smeared with lampblack, so as to make it appear that the finger was missing. His brother stood nodding his head approvingly, his arms folded in his long sleeves. He was made up in such a

185

way as to resemble the other closely.

Suddenly the music stopped. The elder roared something at the second man. He acted as if he were very frightened; he turned round and round, stamping his feet on the stage and rolling his eyes. As the elder shouted again at him, the man took his right hand from his sleeve. His forefinger was missing, too.

The orchestra burst out in a frenzied melody. But the music was nearly drowned in the roar of acclamations from the crowd, Sergeant Hoong joining in at the top of his voice.

"What does it all mean?" Judge Dee asked testily when the din was diminishing.

"It was the husband's twin brother who visited the woman that night!" the sergeant explained hurriedly. "He had cut off his finger, so that the wife would think he was indeed her husband! That's why the piece is entitled 'One Finger for One Night of Spring'!"

"What a story!" Judge Dee said, rising. "We'd better go back." The fat man in front of him was peeling an orange, and throwing the rinds carelessly over his shoulder into Judge Dee's lap.

The stagehands were unrolling a huge red banner inscribed with five large black characters.

"Look, your honor!" Sergeant Hoong said eagerly. "The next piece is 'Three Mysteries Miraculously Solved by Judge Yü'!"

"Well," Judge Dee said, resigned, "Magistrate Yü was the greatest detective of our glorious Han Dynasty, seven hundred years ago. Let's see what they make of that."

Sergeant Hoong sat down again with a contented sigh.

While the orchestra started a vivacious melody punctuated by the clacking of castanets, the stagehands carried a large red table on the stage. A huge figure with a black face and a long beard strode on the

186

stage. He was clad in a flowing black robe embroidered with red dragons and wore a high black cap crowned with a ring of glittering ornaments. He sat down ponderously behind the red table, loudly acclaimed by the enthusiastic spectators.

Two men came up and knelt before the bench. They started a duet sung in a piercing falsetto. Judge Yü listened, combing his beard with his spread-out fingers. He raised his hand, but Judge Dee couldn't see what he pointed at because just at that moment a small ragamuffin selling oil cakes tried to climb over the bench in front of him and got involved in a dispute with the fat man. But by now Judge Dee's ears had become adjusted to the stage diction, and he understood snatches of the song which he could hear above the altercation going on in front of him.

When the small cake vendor had slid away the judge asked Sergeant Hoong, "Aren't those the two brothers again? I think the one accuses the other of having murdered their old father."

The sergeant nodded vigorously. The elder man on the stage rose and pretended to place a small object on the bench. Judge Yü acted as if he took it between thumb and forefinger, scrutinizing it with a deep frown.

"What is that?" Judge Dee asked.

"Haven't you got ears?" the fat man rasped over his shoulder. "It's an almond!"

"I see," Judge Dee said stiffly.

"Their old father," Hoong explained quickly, "left that almond as a clue to his murderer! The elder brother now says that his father wrote the name of the murderer on a piece of paper, concealed inside that almond."

Judge Yü acted as if he carefully unfolded a small piece of paper. Suddenly he produced as if from nowhere a sheet of paper over five feet long, inscribed with two large characters which he showed to the spec-

187

tators. The crowd started to howl indignantly.

"That's the name of the younger brother!" Sergeant Hoong shouted.

"Shut up!" the fat man yelled out at him.

There was a frenzied outburst of the orchestra, gongs, cymbals and small drums striking up together. The younger brother rose and sang a passionate denial of his guilt, accompanied by a strident flute tune. Judge Yü looked from one brother to the other, angrily rolling his eyes. Suddenly the music stopped. In the dead silence that followed Judge Yü leaned forward over the bench, grabbed the lapels of the robes of the two men, and dragged them toward him. He first smelled the mouth of the younger, then that of the elder brother. He roughly pushed the latter away, crashed his fist on the table and shouted something in a thunderous voice. The music struck up again a boisterous tune; the audience burst out in acclamations. The fat man rose and roared, "Good! Good!" at the top of his voice.

"What happened?" Judge Dee asked, interested despite himself.

"The judge said," Sergeant Hoong replied, his goatee quivering with excitement, "that the elder brother smelled of almond milk! The old father knew that his elder son would murder him, and would tamper with whatever clue he would leave. Therefore he put his message inside the almond. The almond was the real clue because the elder brother was very fond of almond milk!"

"Not bad!" Judge Dee remarked. "I had thought that—"

But the orchestra was starting up another deafening piece. Two men dressed in robes glittering with gold were now kneeling before Judge Yü. Each waved in his hands a piece of paper, covered with small writing and with large red seals impressed on it. Judge Dee gathered from their recital that they were two noble-men. Their prince had left each of them half of a large estate, land, houses, slaves and valuables as specified on the papers they were presenting. Each claimed that the division was unjust, and that the other had received more than his proper share.

Judge Yü looked at them, showing the white of his eyes. He angrily shook his head, making the glittering ornaments on his cap dance in the garish light of the lampions. The music grew very soft; there was an atmosphere of tension that communicated itself to Judge Dee.

"Say your piece!" the fat man shouted impatiently.

"Shut up!" Judge Dee heard himself bark, much to his own amazement.

There was a loud clanging of gongs. Judge Yü rose. He grabbed the documents from the hands of the two plaintiffs, then handed to each the other's paper. He raised his hands signifying that the case had been decided. The two noblemen stared perplexedly at the documents in their hands.

A deafening applause rose from the audience. The fat man turned round in his seat. He began in a patronizing tone, "At least you got this, didn't you? You see, those two—"

His voice trailed off. He looked with open mouth at the judge. He had recognized him.

"I understood perfectly, thank you!" the judge said primly. He rose, shook the orange rinds from his lap and started to make his way through the crowd. Sergeant Hoong followed him, casting a last wistful look at the stage, where the actress who had led them to their seats was now appearing before the bench.

"This is the case of a young woman posing as a man, your honor," he said. "Quite a good story!"

"We really must go back now, Hoong," the judge said firmly.

189

While they were walking through the crowded street, Judge Dee suddenly said, "Things usually turn out to be quite different from what one expected, Hoong! I must tell you that when I was still a student, I had envisaged the work of a magistrate to be more or less like that of our old Judge Yü as we saw him just now in action on the stage. I thought I would be behind my bench, condescendingly listening to all kinds of long, confused stories, complicated lies and conflicting statements brought forward by the people before me. Then I would suddenly pounce on the weak point, and deliver judgment then and there, shattering the confused criminal! Well, Hoong, now I know better."

They laughed and continued their stroll back to the tribunal.

Returned to the tribunal, Judge Dee took the sergeant straight to his private office. He said, "Make me a cup of good strong tea, Hoong! And have one yourself too. Then you can lay out my ceremonial robes for the celebration in the White Cloud Temple. It's a nuisance we have to go there. I'd much prefer to stay here and review with you the position regarding our murder case. But it can't be helped!"

When the sergeant had brought the tea, the judge slowly took a few sips. Then he spoke.

"I must say, sergeant, that I now understand your interest in the theatre better. We must go there more often. At first all seems very confused, then the key sentence is spoken, and suddenly all becomes crystal clear. I wish it were the same with our murder case!"

The judge pensively tugged at his mustache.

"That last case," Sergeant Hoong said as he carefully took Judge Dee's ceremonial cap from its leather box, "I have seen before. It concerns the impersonation of—"

Judge Dee didn't seem to have listened. He suddenly hit his fist on the desk.

"Hoong!" he exclaimed, "I think I've got it! August heaven, if that is right, I should have seen it much sooner!"

He thought a few moments, then said, "Get me the district map!"

The sergeant quickly unrolled the large pictorial map for him on the desk. Judge Dee scanned it eagerly, then he nodded.

He jumped up and started pacing the floor, his hands on his back and his shaggy eyebrows knitted in a deep frown.

Sergeant Hoong looked at him tensely. But it was not until the judge had crossed the room scores of times that at last he stood still and said, "That is it! It all fits! Now we must set to work, Hoong. There is much to do, and very little time!"

SEVENTEEN.

A PIOUS ABBOT CONDUCTS A MAGNIFI-
CENT CEREMONY; A SKEPTICAL PHILOS-
OPHER LOSES HIS BEST ARGUMENT

The Rainbow Bridge outside the east gate was illumi-
nated by a row of large lanterns, their colored lights
reflected in the dark water of the creek. The road
leading to the White Cloud Temple was lined by garlands of gaily colored lamps hung from high poles
that had been erected on both sides of the road, and
the temple itself was brilliantly lighted by torches
and oil lamps.

When Judge Dee's palanquin was being carried over
the bridge he saw that there were only very few people
about. The hour set for the ceremony had arrived; the
citizens of Peng-lai had already assembled inside the
temple compound. The judge was accompanied only by
his three assistants and two constables. Sergeant Hoong
sat opposite him inside the palanquin, Ma Joong and
Chiao Tai followed on horseback, and the two constables led the way, carrying on long poles lampions
with the inscription "The Tribunal of Peng-lai."

The palanquin was carried up the broad marble
stairs of the gatehouse. The judge heard the sounds of
cymbals and gongs that punctuated the monotonous
chant of the monks, who were singing a Buddhist
litany in chorus. Through the gate came the heavy
scent of Indian incense.

The main courtyard of the temple was filled by a dense multitude. Overlooking the crowd, on the high terrace in front of the main hall, the abbot was sitting cross-legged on his thronelike seat of red lacquer. He was clad in the violet cassock of his high office, and had a stole of gold brocade round his shoulders. On his left sat the shipowner Koo Meng-pin, the warden of the Korean quarter, and two guild masters, all on lower chairs. The high chair on the abbot's right, the seat of honor, was unoccupied. Next to it sat a captain sent by the commander of the fort, in shining armor and carrying a long sword. Then came Dr. Tsao and two other guild masters.

In front of the terrace a raised platform had been built, and thereon was erected a round altar, richly decorated with silk scarves and fresh flowers. There was enthroned the cedarwood copy of the statue of the Lord Maitreya, under a purple canopy, supported by four gilded pillars.

Round the altar were sitting about fifty monks. Those on the left played various musical instruments, the others formed the chorus. The platform was surrounded by a cordon of lance-knights with shining mail coats and helmets. All around them thronged the crowd; those who had not succeeded in finding a place were precariously perched on the high socles of the pillars that lined the front of the side buildings.

Judge Dee's palanquin was set down at the entrance to the court. A deputation of four elderly monks, resplendent in robes of yellow silk, came to greet him. As the judge was being conducted through the narrow roped-off path leading to the terrace, he noticed among the crowd of onlookers many Chinese and Korean sailors who had come to worship their patron saint.

The judge ascended the terrace, and made a slight bow in front of the small abbot. He told him that pressing official business had caused a delay. The abbot

193

nodded graciously, took his aspersorium and sprinkled the judge with holy water. Then Judge Dee sat down, his three assistants behind his chair. The captain, Koo Meng-pin and the other leading citizens rose and bowed deeply in front of the judge. When they had resumed their seats the abbot gave a sign and the orchestra struck up. The monks of the chorus began chanting a solemn hymn in praise of Buddha.

As the hymn was nearing its end, the large bronze temple bell started booming. On the platform ten monks led by Hui-pen began walking slowly round the altar, swinging their censers. Thick clouds of incense enveloped the statue, which had been burnished to a beautiful shiny dark brown.

Having completed the ceremonial circumambulation, Hui-pen descended from the platform and went up the terrace to the abbot's chair. He knelt and raised above his head a small roll of yellow silk. The abbot leaned forward and accepted the roll from Hui-pen's hands. Hui-pen rose and resumed his place on the platform.

Three beats on the temple bell resounded over the assembly. Then deep silence reigned. The consecration ceremony was going to begin. The abbot would read aloud the prayers inscribed on the yellow roll, then he would sprinkle it with holy water, and finally the roll and some other small ritual objects would be placed in a cavity in the statue's back, thus imparting to it the same mystic virtue possessed by the original sandalwood statue of Maitreya in the cave.

As the abbot started to unroll the yellow scroll, Judge Dee suddenly rose. He went to stand on the edge of the terrace, and slowly surveyed the crowd. All eyes turned to that commanding figure in the long robe of shimmering green brocade. The light of the torches shone on his winged cap of black velvet, seamed with gold. The judge stroked his beard for a while, then put his arms into his wide sleeves. His voice rang out clearly over the assembly as he spoke.

"The imperial government has graciously granted their high protection to the Buddhist Church, inasmuch as its lofty teachings are held to have a beneficial influence on the manners and morals of our myriad black-haired people. It is therefore the duty of me, the magistrate, who represents the imperial government here in Peng-lai, to protect this holy sanctuary, the White Cloud Temple, all the more so since the sacred statue of the Lord Maitreya preserved on its premises guards the lives of our sailors who brave the dangers of the deep."

"Amen!" the small abbot said. At first he had seemed annoyed by the interruption of the ceremony, but now he was nodding his head with a benign smile. He evidently approved of his speech, unannounced as it was.

Judge Dee continued, "Now the shipowner Koo Meng-pin has donated a replica of this sacred statue of the Lord Maitreya, and we are gathered here to witness its solemn consecration. The imperial government has graciously consented that after the ceremony has been completed, the statue shall be conveyed to the imperial capital by a military escort. The government wishes in this manner to show its reverence for a duly consecrated image of a Buddhist deity, and to ensure that nothing untoward will happen to this statue during its transportation to the capital.

"Since I, the magistrate, am fully responsible for all that happens in this officially recognized place of worship, it is my duty to verify, before I give my consent to the consecration, whether this statue is indeed what it is claimed to be, namely a faithful copy carved in cedarwood of the sacred statue of the Lord Maitreya."

A murmur of astonishment rose up from the assembly. The abbot looked dumbfounded at the judge, perplexed by this unexpected ending of what he had supposed to be a congratulatory message. There was some commotion among the monks on the platform. Hui-pen wanted to descend to consult with the abbot, but the soldiers did not let him pass.

Judge Dee raised his hand, and the crowd fell silent again.

"I shall now order my assistant," Judge Dee announced, "to verify the authenticity of this statue."

He gave a sign to Chiao Tai, who quickly went down from the terrace and ascended the platform. Pushing the monks aside, he went in front of the altar and drew his sword.

Hui-pen stepped up to the balustrade. He shouted in a stentorian voice, "Shall we allow this holy statue to be desecrated, risking the terrible wrath of the Lord Maitreya, and thereby imperiling the dear lives of our people at sea?"

An angry roar rose from the crowd. Led by the sailors, they surged forward toward the platform, shouting their protests. The abbot stared at the tall figure of Chiao Tai, his lips parted in fright. Koo, Tsao and the guild masters began whispering to each other anxiously. The captain from the fort worriedly surveyed the excited crowd and his hand went to the hilt of his sword.

Judge Dee raised both his hands.

"Stand back!" he shouted peremptorily at the crowd. "Since this statue has not yet been consecrated it is not entitled to our respect!"

Loud shouts of "Hear and obey!" were heard coming from the entrance to the court. When the people turned their heads they saw that dozens of fully-armed constables and guards of the tribunal were running in.

Chiao Tai felled Hui-pen by hitting him on the head with the flat of his sword. Then he lifted it again and dealt the statue a ferocious blow on its left shoulder. The sword leapt from his hand and clattered to the floor. The statue appeared completely undamaged.

"A miracle!" the abbot shouted ecstatically.

The crowd pressed forward and the lance-knights had to keep them back with their leveled spears.

Chiao Tai jumped down from the platform. The soldiers made way for him and he ran up to the terrace. He handed the judge a small piece his sword had chipped off the shoulder of the statue. Holding the shining sliver up so that all could see it, Judge Dee shouted, "A base fraud has been committed! Impious crooks have insulted the Lord Maitreya!"

Shouting above the din of incredulous voices, he went on.

"This statue is not made of cedarwood, but of solid gold! Greedy criminals wanted thus to convey their smuggled gold to the capital for their illegal gain! I, the magistrate, accuse of this atrocious sacrilege the donor of the statue, Koo Meng-pin, his accomplices, Tsao Ho-hsien and Hui-pen, and declare the abbot and all the other inmates of this temple under arrest, to be heard on the charge of complicity in this sacrilegious crime!"

The crowd kept quiet now; they began to understand the implications of Judge Dee's words. They were impressed by his deep sincerity, and curious to know more about this unexpected development. The captain took his hand from his sword with a sigh of relief.

Judge Dee's voice rang out again.

"I shall now first hear Koo Meng-pin, whom the state accuses of desecration of a recognized place of worship, defrauding the state by smuggling and the murder of an imperial official!"

Two constables dragged Koo from his seat, and pressed him down on his knees at the feet of the judge. He was completely taken by surprise. His face was ashen and he was trembling violently.

Judge Dee addressed him sternly.

"In the tribunal I shall formulate the triple charge against you in great detail. Your evil plot is well known to me. How you clandestinely imported large quantities of gold from Japan and Korea, smuggled that gold to the Korean quarter and thence to this temple, in the form of gold bars concealed inside the staffs of traveling monks. How the accused Tsao Ho-hsien received those loaded staffs in the deserted temple west of the city, and conveyed them to the capital concealed in his book packages. How when his excellency the late Wang Te-hwa, magistrate of this district, became suspicious, you had him murdered by a poison hidden in the roof beam of his library, above his tea stove. And last, how you planned to crown your despicable crimes by casting this statue in solid gold, to be used for your fraudulent manipulations. Confess!"

"I am innocent, your honor!" Koo cried out. "I never knew that this statue was made of gold, and I—"

"Enough of your lies!" Judge Dee barked. "His Excellency Wang told me himself that it was you who planned to murder him! I'll show you his message to me."

The judge took from his sleeve the antique lacquer box that the Korean girl had given to Chiao Tai. He held up its lid, decorated with the pair of golden bamboo stems. Then he resumed.

"You stole the papers inside this box, Koo, and thought that thereby you had obliterated all evidence against you. But little did you know the brilliant mind of your victim. The box itself constitutes the clue! The pair of bamboos depicted on this box points straight at the pair of bamboos of that stick that is your inseparable companion!"

Koo shot a quick look at his stick, standing against his chair. The silver rings that kept the two parallel bamboo stems together glittered in the light of the

198

torches. He silently bowed his head.

The judge continued inexorably, "And the dead magistrate also left other clues, proving that he knew that you were engaged in this nefarious plot, and that it was you who were planning to murder him. I repeat, Koo, confess, and name your accomplices!"

Koo raised his head and stared forlornly at the judge. Then he stammered, "I . . . I confess."

He wiped the perspiration from his brow, then went on in a toneless voice.

"Monks of temples in Korea, traveling in my ships up and down between the Korean ports and Peng-lai, carried the gold bars in their staffs, and Hui-pen and Dr. Tsao were indeed the men who helped me to get the gold from here to the deserted temple, and thence to the capital. Kim Sang assisted me, the almoner Tzu-hai assisted Hui-pen, together with ten other monks whom I shall name. The abbot and the other monks are innocent. The golden statue was cast here under the supervision of Hui-pen, using the fire used for cremating the body of Tzu-hai. The real replica, made by Master Fang, I concealed in my residence. Kim Sang employed a Korean artisan to insert the poison in the roof beam in Magistrate Wang's library, thereafter sent that man back to Korea on the next boat."

Koo raised his head and looked entreatingly at the judge. He cried out, "But I swear that in all these matters I only acted on orders, your honor! The real criminal—"

"Be silent!" Judge Dee ordered him in a thunderous voice. "Don't try to foist new lies on me! Tomorrow you shall have full opportunity for pleading your own cause, in the tribunal." To Chiao Tai he said, "Seize me this man and bring him to the tribunal."

Chiao Tai quickly bound Koo's hands on his back and marched him off, with two constables on either side of him.

Judge Dee pointed at Dr. Tsao, who had remained sitting in his chair as if petrified. But when he saw Ma Joong approaching him he suddenly jumped up and rushed to the other end of the terrace. Ma Joong sprang after him, the doctor tried to duck but Ma Joong caught the end of his flowing beard. Dr. Tsao cried out; his beard came off in Ma Joong's large fist. On the small, receding chin of the doctor there remained only part of a thin strip of plaster, partly ripped off. As he lifted his hands to his bare chin with a howl of despair, Ma Joong caught his wrists and bound them together behind the doctor's back.

A slow smile lit up Judge Dee's stern features. He said to himself with satisfaction, "So that beard was false!"

EIGHTEEN.

THE JUDGE UNCOVERS AN EVIL CONSPIRACY; AN ELUSIVE PERSON IS FINALLY IDENTIFIED

It was long past midnight when Judge Dee and his three assistants came back to the tribunal. The judge took them straight to his private office.

As he sat down behind his desk, Sergeant Hoong hurriedly went to the tea stove on the corner table and prepared a cup of strong tea for him. Judge Dee took a few sips, then leaned back in his chair and spoke.

"Our great statesman and illustrious detective, Governor Yoo Shou-chien, states in his *Instructions to Magistrates* that a detective must never cling stubbornly to one theory, but re-examine it repeatedly as his investigation progresses, and again and again compare it with the facts. And if he finds a new fact that doesn't seem to fit, he must not try to adapt that fact to the theory, but he must either adapt the theory to the fact, or abandon it altogether. I always thought, my friends, that this was so obvious as hardly needing to be mentioned. However, in the case of the murdered magistrate I failed conspicuously to observe this fundamental rule." He smiled wanly as he went on. "Apparently it is not as obvious as I thought!

"When the astute criminal who is at the back of this plot heard that I had applied for the post of magistrate of Peng-lai, he obligingly decided to provide something for me to put my teeth in, in order to keep me busy for a few days. The plans for his final coup, the sending to the capital of the golden statue, were nearing completion. He wanted to put me on a wrong track till the statue would have left Peng-lai. Thus he ordered Koo Meng-pin to lead me astray, and Koo spread the rumor about the arms smuggle. He got that idea from Kim Sang, who had used it already for obtaining the cooperation of the Korean girl. I fell into the trap; the arms smuggle was the basis of all my theorizing. Even after Kim Sang had revealed that it was gold that was being smuggled, I still believed that it was smuggled from China to Korea, although I wondered vaguely how there could be any profit in that. It was only this very night that I saw it was the other way round!"

Judge Dee angrily tugged at his beard. Then, looking at his three assistants, who were eagerly waiting for him to continue, he went on with a bleak smile.

"The only excuse I can adduce for my shortsightedness is that incidental occurrences such as the murder of Fan Choong, the disappearance of Mrs. Koo, and Tang's strange behavior tended to confuse the issue. Further, I concentrated too long on Yee Pen who—quite innocently—came to see me about the rumors of the arms smuggle, and whom I also suspected because of a mistake which I shall explain presently.

"It was the theatrical performance the sergeant took me to earlier tonight that showed me who the magistrate's murderer was. In the theatre piece a man indicated his murderer posthumously by leaving a message in an almond; but the message was only meant to distract the murderer's attention from the real clue, namely the almond itself! Then I suddenly understood that Magistrate Wang had purposely chosen the valuable antique box as container of his papers because the pair of golden bamboo stems on its cover pointed to

Koo's double stick. Since we know that the magistrate was fond of riddles and conundrums, I even suspect that he wanted at the same time to suggest that the gold was being smuggled concealed in bamboo sticks. But that we'll never know.

"Now that I knew that Koo was the murderer, I realized the sinister meaning of the words with which he dismissed Kim Sang before he took me to the crab restaurant; he said, 'You can go on; you know what to do.' Evidently they had already discussed how I could be eliminated as soon as I seemed to be on the right track. And I gave them that idea by foolishly prattling away about monks of the White Cloud Temple using the deserted temple for nefarious purposes, and on top of that mentioning the statue Koo was going to send to the capital! Moreover, during our dinner I tried to make him talk about his wife by vaguely suggesting that she had inadvertently become mixed up in one of his own plans. Koo thought of course that I was giving him to understand that I suspected the truth and that I could arrest him any moment.

"As a matter of fact I then was still very far from the truth, I was worrying about how the smugglers succeeded in getting the gold from the interior to the deserted temple. However, tonight I asked myself what could be the relation between Koo and Dr. Tsao. The doctor had a cousin in the capital, a bibliophile strange to the world who could easily be utilized without suspecting anything wrong. I thought that Dr. Tsao might have helped Koo to get the gold from the capital to Peng-lai by introducing him to his cousin. At that point, at long last, the truth dawned on me, for then I suddenly remembered that Dr. Tsao had been despatching at regular intervals packages of books to the capital. Gold was being smuggled into China, and not the other way round! Thus a ring of clever criminals had assembled a large quantity of cheap gold by evading the high import and road taxes, and were enriching themselves by manipulating the market with that gold.

"At that point, however, I struck a difficulty. The gold scheme could work only if the ring disposed of a tremendous quantity of gold. It is true that it was bought cheap in Korea, but it had to be paid for there, which meant a considerable capital outlay. In order to make really great profits they had to be able to influence the market in the capital, and for that a few score thin staves smuggled in hollow staffs and book packages could never be sufficient. Moreover, by the time I arrived here they apparently no longer used the route I had traced, for Dr. Tsao had already despatched nearly his entire library to the capital. Then I understood the reason for the terrible hurry the criminals were in. Namely that in the very near future a colossal amount of gold was going to be forwarded to the capital. How could that be done? Koo's copy of the statue, to be conveyed to the capital by a government escort, was the obvious answer.

"The supreme effrontery of this audacious plan was worthy of the mastermind who was directing the scheme. At last I understood the meaning of the weird incident Ma Joong and Chiao Tai had witnessed in the mist, on the bank of the canal. I consulted the city map, and saw that Koo's mansion was located near the *first* bridge. I realized that in the mist you two must have misjudged the distance you covered, and thought it was near the *second* bridge that you had witnessed the incident. And it was there that the next day you made your inquiries. Yee Pen lives near there, and that strengthened for a while my suspicions of that unscrupulous but innocent businessman. But apart from that, your eyes hadn't played a trick on you. Only Koo's men didn't club a living man, they broke to pieces the clay model of the statue that Koo had se-

cretly made for casting the mold of the golden statue!
It was that mold that Koo sent to the unsuspecting
abbot of the White Cloud Temple in the rosewood
box. Hui-pen opened the box, and used the cremation
of the body of the almoner as pretext for making the
blazing fire needed for melting the assembled gold
bars and casting the golden statue. I saw with my own
eyes the rosewood box, and I wondered about so great
a fire being necessary for cremating a body. But I suspected nothing. Well, half an hour ago, when we proceeded from the temple to Koo's mansion and searched
it, we found the cedarwood statue made by Master
Fang neatly sawn asunder in a dozen or so pieces.
Those Koo planned to send to the capital, to be put
together there again and offered to the White Horse
Temple, while the golden statue would be brought to
the leader of the scheme. The clay model could easily
be disposed of. It was broken to pieces and dumped
into the canal. Ma Joong stepped on the pieces, with
the paper coating still attached to them."

"Well," Ma Joong said, "I am glad to know that I
still can trust my own eyes. I was getting a bit worried about my having mistaken a basket with garbage
for a sitting man!"

"Why did Dr. Tsao join that criminal scheme, your
honor?" the sergeant asked. "After all, he is a man
of letters, and—"

"Dr. Tsao loved luxury," the judge interrupted. "He
couldn't get over the loss of his money, which forced
him to leave the city and live in that old tower. Everything was false about that doctor, even his beard!
When Koo approached him and promised him a large
share in the profits, he couldn't resist the temptation.
The staff the almoner Tzu-hai was carrying that night
when he met Mrs. Koo and Po Kai contained a bar of
gold, part of the doctor's share he was receiving regularly. Koo made a bad mistake when he let his desire

for Miss Tsao prevail over his caution, and ordered Dr. Tsao to marry her to him. That proved to me that there was a connection between those two men."

Judge Dee sighed. He emptied his teacup, then resumed.

"Koo Meng-pin was an utterly ruthless, greedy man, but he was not the leader of the ring; he had only been acting on orders. But I couldn't let him name his employer. For that man could have other agents here, who would have warned him. This very night—or rather this very morning!—I shall send posthaste to the capital the platoon of mounted military police you saw waiting outside in the courtyard, to forward my accusation of that man to the president of the Metropolitan Court. By the way, their corporal informed me just now that the military police have caught that fellow Woo, Fan's servant, when he was trying to sell the two horses. He had indeed discovered the murder just after Ah Kwang had left the farm. Woo was afraid he would be suspected of having committed the crime, and fled with the cash box and the horses, exactly as we had surmised."

"But who was the archcriminal who led the smuggling scheme, your honor?" Sergeant Hoong asked.

"Of course that treacherous scoundrel Po Kai!" Ma Joong shouted.

Judge Dee smiled.

"As to the sergeant's question," he said, "I really can't answer that, because I don't know who that criminal is. I am waiting for Po Kai to supply me with his name. As a matter of fact, I am wondering why Po Kai hasn't shown up yet. I expected him to come here immediately after our return from the temple."

As his three assistants burst out in astonished questions, there came a knock on the door. The headman rushed inside and reported that Po Kai had calmly walked in through the main gate of the tribunal. The guards had arrested him at once.

"Show him in," the judge said in an even voice. "Without the guards, mind you."

When Po Kai came in the judge quickly rose and bowed.

"Please be seated, Mr. Wang," he said to him politely. "I have been looking forward to this meeting, sir!"

"So have I!" the visitor replied placidly. "Permit me, before we get down to business, to clean up a bit!"

Ignoring the three men who were staring at him dumbfounded, he walked over to the tea stove, took a towel from the hot water basin and carefully rubbed his face. When he turned round, the purple spots that gave his face its bloated appearance and the red nose-tip had vanished, and his eyebrows were now thin and straight. He took a round piece of black plaster from his sleeve and stuck that on his left cheek.

Ma Joong and Chiao Tai gasped. That was the face they had seen in the coffin. They both exclaimed at the same time.

"The dead magistrate!"

"His twin brother," Judge Dee corrected them, "Mr. Wang Yuan-te, senior secretary of the Board of Finance." To Wang he continued, "That birthmark must have saved you and your brother much embarrassment, sir, not to speak of your parents!"

"It has indeed," Wang answered. "Apart from that, we were as much alike as two peas in a pod. After we had grown up it didn't matter any more, though, for then my poor brother was serving in the provinces, while I always remained in the Board of Finance. Not many people knew indeed that we were twins. But that is neither here nor there. I came to thank you, magistrate, for your brilliant solution of my brother's murder, and for supplying me with the data I needed for righting the false accusation his murderer brought forward against me in the capital. I was present at the gathering in the temple tonight, disguised as a monk, and heard how you have successfully unraveled this complicated plot, while I never got further than vague suspicions."

"I suppose," Judge Dee asked eagerly, "that Koo's employer is a high official in the capital?"

Wang shook his head.

"No," he replied. "It is a fairly young man, but very old in depravity. A junior secretary in the Metropolitan Court called Hou, the nephew of our secretary-general, Hou Kwang."

The judge grew pale.

"Secretary Hou?" he exclaimed. "He is one of my friends!"

Wang shrugged his shoulders.

"Often," he remarked, "one makes mistakes in judging one's closest friends. Young Hou is a gifted man. In due course he would certainly have risen high in official life. But he thought he could find a short cut to wealth and influence by swindling and deceiving, and when he saw that he had been discovered, he did not hesitate to commit a base murder. He was very favorably placed for evolving his evil schemes. For through his uncle he knew everything about the affairs of our Board of Finance, while as a secretary of the Court he had access to all documents there. It was he who was the leader of the plot."

Judge Dee passed his hand over his eyes. Now he understood why Hou, when six days before he had seen him off in the Pavilion of Joy and Sadness, had insisted so much on his giving up the plan of proceeding to Peng-lai. He remembered the look of entreaty he had seen in Hou's eyes. At least Hou's friendship for him had not been entirely feigned. And now it was he who had brought about Hou's downfall. This thought took away all the elation he had felt about his solution of the case. He asked Wang in a toneless voice, "How did you obtain the first clue to this plot?"

"Heaven has granted me a special sense for figures," Wang replied. "It is to that gift that I owe my quick promotion in the Board. One month ago I began to notice discrepancies in the statements on our gold market drawn up regularly by the Board. I suspected that cheap gold was entering the country illegally. I started an investigation of my own, but unfortunately my clerk must have been a spy for Hou. Since Hou knew that my brother was magistrate here in Peng-lai, the source of his smuggled gold, he—quite wrongly—concluded that my brother and I were working together on exposing him. As a matter of fact, my brother had written me only once about some suspicions of his that Peng-lai was a center of smuggling, I had not connected that vague information with the gold manipulations in the capital. But Hou made the mistake of many criminals, he assumed too soon that he had been discovered, and took precipitate action. He ordered Koo to murder my brother, and he had the clerk killed. He took thirty bars of gold from the Treasury, and had his uncle accuse me of those crimes. I succeeded in fleeing before I was arrested, and came to Peng-lai disguised as Po Kai, in order to discover evidence of Hou's scheme and thus avenge my brother's murder, and at the same time clear myself of the false accusation.

"Your arrival here placed me in a difficult position. I would have liked to co-operate with you but could not reveal my identity, for then it would of course have been your duty to arrest me at once and forward me to the capital. But I did what I could in an indirect way. I approached your two assistants and took them to the floating brothels in order to interest them in Kim Sang and the Korean girl, whom I suspected. In that I succeeded fairly well." He gave Chiao

Tai a quick glance. The tall fellow hastily buried his face in his teacup. "I also tried to draw their attention to the Buddhist crowd—but in that I was less successful. I suspected that the monks were concerned in the gold smuggle, but couldn't discover any clues. I kept a close watch on the White Cloud Temple; the floating brothels were a useful observation post. I saw the almoner Tzu-hai leave the temple in a stealthy way and followed him, but unfortunately he died before I could interrogate him about what he was going to do in the deserted temple.

"I questioned Kim Sang a bit too closely and he became suspicious of me. That is why he did not oppose my coming along on the boat trip; he thought he might as well kill me too." Turning to Ma Joong, he said, "During the fight on the barge they made the mistake of concentrating on you. They considered me a negligible quantity, and planned to finish me off later at leisure. But I am rather handy with a knife, and stuck it in the back of the man who grabbed you from behind when the fight started."

"That certainly was a timely gesture!" Ma Joong said gratefully.

"When I had heard Kim Sang's last words," Wang pursued, "and thus knew that my suspicions about the gold smuggle were correct, I took the dinghy and hurried back at once to get my box which contained amongst other notes those on Hou's trumped-up charge against me and on his market manipulations—before Kim Sang's accomplices would steal them from my room in Yee Pen's house. Since they suspected 'Po Kai,' I decided to drop that disguise, and adopted that of an itinerant monk."

"Seeing all the wine we have swilled together," Ma Joong growled, "you could at least have said a few words of explanation before leaving the barge."

"A few words wouldn't have sufficed," Wang replied

dryly. To Judge Dee he remarked, "Those two are a useful pair, if somewhat rough-mannered. Are they in your permanent service?"

"They certainly are," the judge replied.

Ma Joong's face lit up. Nudging Chiao Tai, he said, "The marching with frozen toes up and down the northern frontier is off, brother!"

"I chose the disguise of Po Kai," Wang continued, "because I knew that if I posed as a dissolute poet and fervent Buddhist, I would sooner or later come into contact with the same persons my brother had associated with. And as an eccentric drunkard I could roam over the city all times of day and night without arousing suspicion."

"The part you acted was well chosen," Judge Dee said. "I shall now draw up the charge against Hou, and a platoon of the military police shall bring it at once to the capital. Since the murder of a magistrate is a crime against the state, I can bypass the prefect and the governor and address it directly to the president of the Metropolitan Court. He'll have Hou arrested at once. Tomorrow I shall hear Koo, Tsao, Huipen and the monks involved in the plot, and as soon as possible send the full report on the case to the capital. As a matter of form I shall have to keep you under detention here in the tribunal, sir, pending the official notice that the charges against you have been withdrawn. This will give me the opportunity for profiting by your advice on the financial technicalities of the case, while I also hope to consult you on an eventual simplification of the land taxes in this district. I studied the dossier on that subject and it struck me that the tax burden of the small peasants is unduly heavy."

"I am completely at your service," Wang said. "By the way, how did you identify me? I thought I would have to explain everything to you."

"When I met you in the corridor of your brother's

house," Judge Dee replied. "I suspected that you were the murderer, who had disguised himself as his victim's ghost in order to be able to search undisturbed for incriminating material the dead magistrate might have left. So strong was that suspicion that the same night I paid a secret visit to the White Cloud Temple, and had a look at your brother's corpse. But then I saw that the likeness was too perfect ever to be achieved by artificial means. Thus I was convinced I had really seen the dead magistrate's ghost.

"It was only tonight that I hit on the truth. I saw a theatre piece about twin brothers who could be told apart only by the missing forefinger of one of them. That made me doubt the reality of the ghost, for I reflected that if the dead man had had a twin brother, he could easily have posed as his ghost, perhaps by sticking or painting a birthmark on his cheek, if that were necessary. And Tang told me that the dead man's only living relative was a brother, who had as yet failed to get in touch with the tribunal. 'Po Kai' was the only man who could qualify: he had arrived here directly after the magistrate's murder, he was interested in the case, and Miss Tsao and an observant waiter had made me suspect that he was acting a part.

"If, sir, your name hadn't happened to be Wang— together with Li and Djang occurring most frequently among our people—I might have placed you earlier. For at the time when I was leaving the capital, your alleged crimes and your disappearance were creating quite a stir there. As it was, 'Po Kai's' remarkable skill in financial matters finally supplied the clue. It made me think that he might be connected with the Board of Finance, and then it struck me at last that both the murdered magistrate and the absconding secretary of the Board bore the same surname, Wang."

The judge heaved a sigh. He pensively caressed his side whiskers for a while, then resumed.

"A more experienced magistrate would doubtless have unraveled this case sooner, sir. But this is my first post, I am only a beginner." Opening his drawer, he took out the notebook and handed it to Wang, saying, "Even now I don't understand the meaning of the notes your brother made here."

Wang slowly leafed through the notebook, and studied the figures. Then he said, "I didn't approve of my brother's slack morals, but it can't be denied that he could be very shrewd when he chose. This is a detailed record of the incoming ships of Koo's firm, with the amounts of harbor dues, import taxes and the head taxes of the passengers he paid. My brother must have found out that the import taxes were so low that Koo could hardly have imported sufficient cargo to cover his costs, while the head taxes were so high that his ships must have carried an abnormally large quantity of passengers. That excited his suspicion and made him think of smuggling. My brother was lazy by nature, but if he happened to meet with something that tickled his curiosity, he would study it wholeheartedly and shun no labor to find the solution. He was already that way when he was a boy. Well, this was the last puzzle my poor brother solved."

"Thank you," Judge Dee said. "That disposes of my last problem. And you also solved for me the problem of the ghostly apparition."

"I knew that if I acted the part of my dead brother's ghost," Wang remarked, "I could make investigations in the tribunal without anybody daring to challenge me if I was discovered. I could go freely in and out there, because shortly before his demise my brother sent me a key to the back door of his residence. Apparently he had a foreboding about his impending death, as proved also by his entrusting the lacquer box to that Korean girl. The investigator surprised me when I was searching my brother's library, and the old scribe saw

213

me when I was looking for my brother's private papers in this office. You I also met quite by accident when I was examining my brother's luggage. Allow me to offer you my sincere apologies for my rude behavior on that occasion!"

Judge Dee smiled bleakly.

"They are gladly accepted!" he replied. "All the more so since last night in the White Cloud Temple, when you appeared before me the second time in your ghostly disguise, you saved my life. I must say, though, that on that second occasion you did indeed frighten me very much, your hand looked quite transparent, and you seemed to dissolve suddenly into the mist. How did you achieve that macabre effect?"

Wang had been listening to the judge with mounting astonishment. Now he spoke perplexedly.

"You say I appeared before you a second time? You must be mistaken! I never went to the temple as my dead brother's ghost."

In the deep silence that followed these words there came from somewhere in the building the faint sound of a door being closed, this time very softly.